W9-BYS-366

UNDER THEIR SKIN

Also by Margaret Peterson Haddix

THE MISSING

Found

Sent

Sabotaged

Torn

Caught

Risked

Revealed

Redeemed

Sought (an e-Book original)

Rescued (an e-Book original)

THE SHADOW CHILDREN

Among the Hidden

Among the Impostors

Among the Betrayed

Among the Barons

Among the Brave

Among the Enemy

Among the Free

THE PALACE CHRONICLES

Just Ella

Palace of Mirrors

Palace of Lies

The Girl with 500 Middle Names

Because of Anya

Say What?

Dexter the Tough

Running Out of Time

Full Ride

Game Changer

The Always War

Claim to Fame

Uprising

Double Identity

The House on the Gulf

Escape from Memory

Takeoffs and Landings

Turnabout

Leaving Fishers

Don't You Dare Read This, Mrs. Dunphrey

MARGARET PETERSON
HADDIX

UNDER THEIR SKIN

Simon & Schuster Books for Young Readers
NEW YORK • LONDON • TORONTO • SYDNEY • NEW DELHI

SIMON & SCHUSTER BOOKS FOR YOUNG READERS
An imprint of Simon & Schuster Children's Publishing Division
1230 Avenue of the Americas, New York, New York 10020
This book is a work of fiction. Any references to historical events, real people, or real places are used fictitiously. Other names, characters, places, and events are products of the author's imagination, and any resemblance to actual events or places or persons, living or dead, is entirely coincidental.
Text copyright © 2016 by Margaret Peterson Haddix
Jacket illustration copyright © 2016 by Shane Rebenshied
All rights reserved, including the right of reproduction in whole or in part in any form.
SIMON & SCHUSTER BOOKS FOR YOUNG READERS is a trademark of Simon & Schuster, Inc
For information about special discounts for bulk purchases, please contact Simon & Schuster Special Sales at 1-866-506-1949 or business@simonandschuster.com.
The Simon & Schuster Speakers Bureau can bring authors to your live event.
For more information or to book an event, contact the Simon & Schuster Speakers Bureau at 1-866-248-3049 or visit our website at www.simonspeakers.com.
Jacket design by Krista Vossen
Interior design by Hilary Zarycky
The text for this book is set in Electra.
Manufactured in the United States of America
1215 FFG
2 4 6 8 10 9 7 5 3 1
Library of Congress Cataloging-in-Publication Data
Haddix, Margaret Peterson.
Under Their Skin / Margaret Peterson Haddix.—First edition.
pages cm
Summary: Twelve-year-old twins Nick and Eryn investigate why their mother and new stepfather are keeping secrets, why they are forbidden to meet their stepsiblings, and, most important, why their lives are in danger.
ISBN 978-1-4814-1758-7 (hardcover)
ISBN 978-1-4814-1760-0 (eBook)
[1. Science fiction. 2. Robots–Fiction. 3. Human being—Fiction. 4. Extinction (Biology)—Fiction. 5. Secrets—Fiction. 6. Twins—Fiction. 7. Brothers and sisters—Fiction.] I. Title.
PZ7.H1164Rdm 2016
[Fic]—dc23
2014036962

For anyone who's ever had a sister, a brother,
a stepbrother, a stepsister,
a mother, a father,
a stepfather, a stepsister,
or any other kind of family.

ONE

"You're doing WHAT?" Nick exploded.

"Getting married again," Mom said calmly. She took a sip of her coffee. "People do it all the time."

"Not you," Nick said. "You don't. You're too—"

Eryn had to kick him under the breakfast table. She was pretty sure his next word was going to be *weird.* Or *strange.* Or *too much of an oddball.*

It wasn't that Eryn thought she could read Nick's mind because they were twins. She was just good at figuring people out.

This morning she'd known the minute she woke up that something unusual was happening. Even from her snug cocoon of a bed, she'd been able to smell Mom's turkey-sausage-and-egg-substitute casserole. Mom only made that casserole for special occasions, like Christmas morning. And . . .

Okay, only Christmas, Eryn thought. In her entire

twelve years of life, Eryn couldn't think of a single other time Mom had made that casserole. But every December 25, Mom made two pans of it: one to have with Nick and Eryn, and one for Dad to take to Grandma and Grandpa's after he dropped off Nick and Eryn.

Mom and Dad had been divorced since Eryn and Nick were babies, but it was what they called an "amicable" divorce. Everybody was nice to everybody else.

But now if Mom's getting married again, will everything change? Eryn wondered. *Is that why Mom wants us to think today is as special as Christmas? So we start out with a good attitude?*

Eryn looked down at the table in front of her. Besides the special breakfast casserole, there was also a pan of the cinnamon rolls that Mom usually made only for Nick and Eryn's birthday. The orange juice in the glasses looked fresh-squeezed.

And even though it was a Saturday morning, it kind of seemed like Mom had dressed up for breakfast. Mom wasn't the type to lounge around in sweatpants, anyhow, so it was hard to tell. But the wool blazer, silk blouse, and perfectly styled hair were over the top even for Mom.

Eryn realized that Nick was glaring at her with an expression that clearly said, *Okay, genius, if you don't like what I was going to say, why don't you do the talking?*

Sometimes they did kind of have twin telepathy.

Eryn took a tiny sip of her juice. Yep, it had definitely been surrounded by orange peel only a few minutes ago.

"Um, congratulations, Mom," Eryn said, trying to sound enthusiastic. "That's great! I bet you and Michael will be really happy together!"

She darted her eyes at Nick as if to say, *There. That's the best I can do. It's your turn. Just don't say you think Michael is weird too. Even though he is.*

Really, weren't all adults pretty weird?

Mom blinked in her usual slow, thoughtful way.

"I know you're both wondering how this will affect your lives," she said. "Because you are preteens. And preteens, facing all the changes of adolescence, are predisposed to be a little self-obsessed."

This really was how Mom talked. She was a middle-school psychologist—she got paid to talk like that.

"No, no, we're just happy for you . . . ," Eryn said, forgetting she'd planned to let Nick speak next.

Mom blinked again. When she was little, Eryn had asked Mom once if all that blinking was a sign that her brain was turning off and on. Or switching channels. Mom had laughed so hard at that.

"Nonsense," Mom said. "It's perfectly normal to be concerned about your own well-being. I won't lie to you. You will have to adjust to some big changes. But I think they are changes that will enrich your lives."

Nick stabbed his fork into his turkey sausage.

"Michael will be around a lot more," he said. "Right? That's a change." He glanced at Eryn. "But—that's okay. I like Michael."

Mom let Nick play video games when Michael was around. Somehow Eryn didn't think Mom meant more of that would be "enriching."

What if, once they're married, Michael thinks he gets to tell us what to do all the time? Eryn wondered. *What if he starts yelling at Nick for playing video games? Or tells me I have to play too? What if he thinks he gets to tell us to do our homework and clean our rooms?*

"After the wedding, Michael will be here all the time, right?" Eryn asked, trying not to sound like she thought that would be disastrous. "He'll move in with us?" Something worse occurred to her. "He wouldn't expect *us* to move in with *him*, would he?"

She had never actually been to Michael's condo. Mom had always had a policy of not letting Nick and Eryn spend much time with anyone she dated. Dad did the same thing. It had something to do with child psychology, and with Mom and Dad not wanting Nick and Eryn to get too attached to someone who might not be around very long. Since Nick and Eryn spent every other week at Mom's and every other week at Dad's, this always worked out. But Mom and Michael had been dating for two years. Now that Eryn thought about it, wasn't it kind of weird that she and Nick had never seen where Michael lived?

When he was going to become their stepfather?

There. Eryn had let herself think the dreaded word.

Mom patted Eryn's shoulder.

"Don't worry," Mom said. "Michael and I discussed where we're going to live, and we want to make sure we're fair to everyone. We don't want to make it like anyone is moving into anyone else's turf. That's why we're going to buy a house that's totally new to everyone."

"What?" Nick exploded once again. He dropped his fork and bolted half out of his chair. "We're *moving*?"

This time Eryn didn't kick him under the table.

"But, but . . . ," Eryn sputtered. "We've lived here our whole lives! Our whole lives when we aren't at Dad's, I mean! Which I guess is our whole lives half the time, but . . ."

It wasn't like Eryn to be at a loss for words, but she was now.

"I was hoping we could have this discussion calmly, and you could fully adjust to thinking about only one change at a time," Mom said. "But yes. We're going to move."

Mom gently maneuvered Nick back into his chair. She kept her hand firmly on his shoulder. She put her other hand back on Eryn's shoulder, too, keeping her in place.

"Don't worry," Mom said. "We're doing everything we can to keep any negative impact on the two of you to a minimum. We'll stay in Maywood, so you won't have to change schools. And we'll look for a house that's no more than ten or fifteen minutes away from your dad's house. So sure, we'll live in a different *structure*, but nothing else of any importance will change."

Sometimes Eryn felt like she had to translate Mom's school-psychologist gobbledygook in her head. Sometimes that meant it took her brain a while to catch up with Mom's words.

This was one of those times.

"Wait a minute," Eryn said, shaking Mom's hand off her shoulder. "You said something about only one change at a time. You're getting married, we're moving—what else are you going to spring on us?"

Mom opened her mouth, but it felt like a full minute passed before anything came out.

"*Can't* we just take this one change at a time?" she asked faintly.

"Oh no," Nick said. "What else is there?"

He was looking at Eryn, not Mom. His dark brown eyes drilled into her identically dark brown eyes. At times like this, Eryn didn't feel like they were just twins. They were teammates. They were partners. They were two halves of the same brain.

It was them against Mom.

"What else could there be?" Eryn asked, waving her arms dramatically. "What else happens when you get a stepdad? It's not like Michael has kids, so we won't have to deal with stepbrothers or stepsisters. Or—"

Mom made the tiniest sound in the back of her throat, and Eryn whirled on her.

"Mom?" Eryn said.

"*Does* Michael have kids?" Nick asked.

"Kids you've somehow never bothered telling us about?" Eryn added.

Mom pursed her lips. She blinked three times.

"Well, actually, um . . . yes," she said. Her tone changed, switching to her *I'm the mom, and I'm in charge—don't question me* voice. Her *sweep everything under the rug* voice. "Michael does have kids. But don't worry. I promise, you'll never have to meet them."

TWO

This is a setup, Nick thought.

He could still remember Mom using reverse psychology on him to get him to brush his teeth or take a bath or go to bed when he was a little kid. After dinner every night she'd say, "Now, Nick, I know you want to go brush your teeth right now, but you are absolutely *not* allowed. You need to wait at least an hour. I'm sorry, but getting ready for bed is simply not permitted yet." And, stupid little kindergartner that he was, Nick would race to the bathroom and grab his toothbrush and scrub it against his teeth as hard as he could.

This is the exact same thing, Nick thought. *Mom thinks we're going to start begging, "Oh, please, we* want *stepbrothers and stepsisters! We want a million of them! Please let us meet them!"*

Wouldn't it be funny if Nick just said, "Yo, Mom,

we're twelve. Not five. Ain't gonna fall for none of that. Uh-uh"?

Mom didn't have much of a sense of humor, but he could probably make Eryn laugh.

Except Eryn did seem to be falling for Mom's setup. Eryn was going totally ape.

"Mom, what are you talking about?" Eryn screeched, shaking her head so hard that her shoulder-length brown hair flew out in all directions. "Who are these kids? How old are they? Where have they been all this time?"

She barely paused to give Mom a chance to answer, but Mom's face was already set like stone. The information about Michael's kids might as well be locked away in a vault.

"You and Michael have been dating for *two years*," Eryn wailed. "How could Michael have had kids all along that neither of you even *mentioned*? What kind of dad is he that he never once said something like, 'Oh, my little Billy likes that kind of ice cream too?' Or, 'Want to help me pick out a birthday present for my little Katie?' He never even spoke their *names* around us! You *still* haven't told us their names. Or—anything!"

Nick leaned forward and tried to catch his sister's eye. She didn't seem to notice.

"And . . . and . . . having stepsiblings we never meet?" Eryn went on ranting. "That's just *weird*, Mom. People don't *do* that."

Mom stood up and took Eryn by the shoulders. She fixed her eyes on Eryn's face and spoke in a calm, emotionless voice.

"Young lady," Mom said, "we have talked about this and talked about this. And we will continue talking about this as long as you are susceptible to peer pressure. You shouldn't be so concerned with what other people do or don't do, or what they might think of you and your actions. You have to make the right decision for *you*, which may or may not be what others choose. And as a family, we have to do what's right for us. We think about our impact on others, of course, and on society as a whole, but . . ."

Nick tuned out. He'd heard this lecture before. He gave up trying to get Eryn's attention and brought a forkful of turkey sausage to his mouth. He might as well eat while he waited for Eryn to figure out Mom's trick.

"But, Mom, why?" Eryn wailed. "Whether it's normal or not—and it isn't—*why* don't you want us to meet these other kids?"

Mom blinked, almost as if she hadn't expected this question.

"Stepsibling relationships can be very challenging in a blended family," she said. She seemed to be speaking with great care. "Ava and Jackson have absolutely nothing in common with you and Nick. Michael and I have decided that it simply wouldn't be fair to any of you to expect you to integrate into a single family unit, especially at a time when you're facing so many other changes. So we'll keep you totally apart. Ava and Jackson will be at their mother's house while you two are with Michael and me, and you'll be at Dad's whenever Ava and Jackson are around. We feel that this is best for everyone."

Red alert! Red alert! Nick thought, almost choking on his sausage.

This had to be the bait in Mom's trap. She had everything set up for Eryn to wail, *But, Mom! You've always told us people can be totally different and still be BFFs! Are you saying you don't think we could love a stepbrother or stepsister who's different?* Or she could say, *Hello? Do* Nick *and I have anything in common except being born together?* Or . . .

Nick decided he needed to stop thinking of things Eryn might say and just stop her from taking the bait. He stretched out his leg under the table, to give her the same kind of kick she'd given him. But his aim was a little off. His foot slammed into one of the table legs. The whole table shook, and orange juice sloshed out of all three glasses.

"Who did that—Nick?" Mom cried, jumping back so none of the juice landed on her tan pants.

"Sorry, sorry," Nick said quickly. "Remember how my legs are growing faster than I can keep track of? I'll clean it up."

He went into the kitchen and waited just a split second.

"Hey, Eryn, can you help me find the dishcloth?" he called.

He wasn't looking out into the breakfast nook, but he was pretty sure Eryn would roll her eyes at that. He didn't care as long as she still came into the kitchen. He leaned over the sink, pretending he was searching hard.

A moment later, Eryn stomped up behind him.

"Seriously, Nick? It's right in front of you," she said, lifting the cloth from the dish drainer, wetting it under the faucet, and wringing it out.

Nick used the sound of the running water as cover.

"I needed to warn you," he whispered. "She's using reverse psychology. Don't fall for it."

Eryn squinted at him. Her squints were like Mom's blinks—that's what they each did when they were thinking.

Eryn squinted so much she would probably have permanent lines on her face by the time she was twenty.

Quickly, Eryn glanced back toward Mom in the breakfast nook and said loudly, "Oh, come on, Nick. You need to rinse it out better than that."

She turned the water back on, full force and loud. But she didn't put the dishcloth under the faucet.

"I don't think that's what she's up to," she whispered back to Nick. "I'll be careful, but . . . there's something else going on. Something suspicious. And I'm going to figure out what it is."

Nick shrugged and grimaced and hoped Eryn would figure out that he meant, *All right. But don't say I didn't warn you.*

Eryn shut off the water, and both of them went back to the breakfast nook. Nick started wiping up the spilled orange juice.

Eryn slid back into her chair.

"Okay, I get that us being at Dad's half the time and those other kids being at their mom's half the time means we don't actually have to live together," Eryn said. "And believe me, that's *fine*. But you said we'd never even *meet* them. How about at the wedding? Aren't you inviting your own children to your wedding?"

Mom daintily dabbed her mouth with her napkin.

"Actually, no," she said. "Sorry. We're eloping. Michael and I decided it would be so much more romantic to elope."

Nick aimed a kick at Eryn again. He tried to make it more accurate this time. But at the same time, apparently Eryn was trying to kick him.

Their feet met in the middle, under the table, and that was all they needed.

Eryn's kick very clearly said, *Eloping? Who are they kidding? They're both, like, forty! Now do you believe me that something weird is going on? Will you help me figure out what it is?*

Nick's kick carried a briefer message: *Oh yeah.*

THREE

Ava and Jackson, Eryn thought. *Jackson and Ava.*

It had been thirty-six hours since Mom had sprung the news on her and Nick about the marriage, the move, and the mystery stepsiblings. And in those thirty-six hours, that was all Eryn had been able to find out about the mysterious kids: their names.

No matter how much she and Nick asked, Mom wouldn't tell them anything else.

They'd even Googled the two kids' names and found nothing.

Now it was Sunday night, and Dad had just arrived to pick them up for the next week at his house. Eryn met him at the front door.

"Did you know?" she demanded.

Dad looked baffled. He hit the palm of his hand against the side of his head, which was his jokey way of acting like he was trying to jar something loose in his brain. This left his wild, curly, dark hair slightly mashed on one side.

"Um . . . know what, Sunshine?" he asked.

Mom slid up behind Eryn and held the door open for Dad.

"Hi, Donald," she said, giving him a single kiss on the right cheek. He responded by giving her a single kiss on the left cheek.

This was their Sunday night routine. Once, years ago, Eryn had talked herself into thinking Mom and Dad might get back together. She only had the nerve to tell this theory to Nick. But somehow, even as a six- or seven-year-old, Nick had been cued in enough to adult behavior to tell her, "They kiss on the *cheek*. People who want to get married kiss on the *mouth*."

Now Eryn could see that her parents' Sunday night kiss routine was about as romantic as oatmeal. It was like flossing their teeth or vacuuming the carpet: a duty.

But when Mom and Michael are married, are Nick and I going to have to see those two kissing all the time? Eryn wondered. *Constantly being romantic and lovey-dovey? Ugh!*

She distracted herself from this new, distressing image in her head by listening to Mom and Dad.

Mom was telling Dad, "I assume Eryn is referring to my getting married."

Mom turned to face Eryn directly.

"Yes, honey, of course I already told your father," she said. "It would be highly inconsiderate of me not to keep him informed of any upcoming change that would affect you and Nick so dramatically."

While Mom wasn't looking, Dad rolled his eyes at Eryn. But it was in a jokey, good-natured way, so even if Mom saw him, her feelings wouldn't be hurt.

"Abso-dutely-lutely, Eryn," Dad said. "She told me. And I have already wished her and Michael many, many years of happiness together."

If Dad had ever had any hopes of getting back together with Mom, he was good at hiding it. He really did sound happy for Mom and Michael.

Mom and Dad went into Mom's office. This was also part of their Sunday night routine. The parent who'd had Nick and Eryn the previous week always told the parent who would have them the following week what tests they had coming up, what school projects were due when, and what extracurricular activities were on the schedule. At least, that was what Mom and Dad claimed happened in their weekly meetings. Eryn guessed that

Mom usually did most of the talking no matter who'd had the kids last.

Nick flopped down on the couch and picked up a video controller. This was *his* Sunday night routine: He was allowed to play video games for as long as Mom and Dad were in Mom's office.

Eryn inched closer to Mom's office door.

"Give it up," Nick said, his eyes glued to the TV screen. "They have to know you might eavesdrop. They're not going to say anything about those kids. Or anything else important."

"Then why don't they just talk in front of us?" Eryn asked.

"Divorced parents need to meet regularly in an environment where they can express their thoughts and emotions freely, with no fear of those thoughts and emotions damaging their children's psyches," Nick said in an airy, *how could you not know this?* tone. Eryn couldn't tell if he was quoting Mom exactly or just pretending to.

"At least I'm trying *something*," Eryn retorted.

"Hey, I'm saving a frog from death-by-delivery-truck," Nick said, as the familiar *ga-lumph, ga-lumph* of his favorite video game started up.

Eryn put her ear against the office door. Nothing.

"I read somewhere that it helps to put a glass up against a wall," Nick said. "Something about concentrating the sound waves."

"Why don't we both try?" Eryn suggested.

Nick didn't move anything except a finger on the video game controller.

"They would know something was up if they came out of the office and I *wasn't* sitting in front of the TV," he said.

He had a point. Eryn went into the kitchen and pulled a glass from the cupboard. She came back into the living room and put the open end of the glass against the wall, then her ear against the base of the glass.

". . . so then Nick has lacrosse practice after school on Tuesday while Eryn has art club," Mom was saying on the other side of the wall. It sounded a little bit like she was talking underwater, but Eryn could still make out the words.

"It works!" Eryn mostly mouthed/sort of whispered to Nick.

She didn't tell him that it seemed like he was right, and Mom and Dad weren't saying anything interesting. Nick always had lacrosse practice the same time as her art club. And she always had tennis practice on Thursdays while he had trumpet lessons. And on Fridays she had piano lessons while he worked on stage crew for the school play.

Wonder what activities Ava and Jackson are in? she thought.

Did it matter? Would that explain who they really were? Were they even old enough to be involved in school activities? Were they even old enough to be in school?

Mom's voice was droning on in the office.

"Wednesday is the field trip to the science museum for both kids, and . . ."

Eryn was just about ready to slide the glass away from the wall so she didn't get caught. Then she heard Dad say, "Don't you think we've been boring long enough, and anyone who might be listening has given up?"

They expected *me to listen?* Eryn wondered.

Then she heard Dad's next words: "Is the plan working so far?"

"As far as we can tell," Mom said.

Plan? Eryn thought. *What plan?*

Maybe Mom was just talking about the wedding plans—or the elopement plans—but Dad made it sound like a plan he was involved with too.

"Don't take too many risks," Dad said.

Mom gave a shaky laugh.

"Isn't everything about this risky?" she said. "But—worth the risks?"

Would Mom talk that way about getting remarried? Would she talk that way to *Dad* about her marriage to Michael?

"Just . . . don't do anything to endanger Eryn and Nick," Dad said in a grim voice that was nothing like his usual light, joking tone.

"You know I never would," Mom said. She paused. "But don't you know we have to factor Ava and Jackson into the equation now too? Don't they matter just as much?"

There was a creaking sound that Eryn recognized—Mom must be rolling her chair back from her desk. Quickly Eryn pulled her glass back from the wall and began carrying it toward the kitchen.

The door to Mom's office swung open before Eryn had a chance to take three steps.

Eryn thought fast. She held the glass up so Mom and Dad were sure to see it.

"Look at what a slob Nick was," she said. "Leaving dirty glasses all over the house. . . . Are Michael's kids this messy?"

"That's not really any of your concern," Mom said, with a shrug that seemed almost rehearsed. "But I appreciate you cleaning up after Nick."

They don't even suspect, Eryn thought. *I got away with eavesdropping!*

But the eavesdropping meant she had questions she couldn't ask now.

Were she and Nick in danger? From what?

Would it be dangerous for them even to *meet* Ava and Jackson?

How could that be?

FOUR

Nick's theory was, if you wanted to trick one of your parents into telling you a secret, you should try the parent who *didn't* have a PhD in psychology.

Now he and Eryn were in the car with Dad, headed to Dad's house. Nick had made sure that Eryn was in the backseat and he was in the front with Dad. Ever since she'd eavesdropped on Mom and Dad, every time the grown-ups weren't looking, Eryn kept peering at Nick and wiggling her eyebrows up and down and mouthing words like *I found something out! Just wait until I tell you!*

Dad could be kind of clueless sometimes, but even he would be able to tell Eryn was up to something if she was sitting right beside him.

"So—good week at Mom's?" Dad asked, pulling to a stop at a red light and glancing over at Nick. It was kind of a silly question, because Dad always called on Mondays, Wednesdays, and Fridays when Eryn and Nick were staying at Mom's. (Mom always called on Tuesdays, Thursdays, and Saturdays when the kids were at Dad's.) So Dad already knew pretty much everything that had happened to Eryn and Nick last week.

This didn't stop Eryn from leaning forward from the backseat and blurting out, "We're kind of weirded out about Mom getting married again, and us moving and getting a new brother and sister. . . ."

Nick shot his sister a look that said, *Ever heard of subtlety? Let me handle this one!*

Eryn frowned, but eased back into her seat.

"You like Michael okay, right?" Nick asked Dad.

"Oh yeah," Dad said, and it sounded like he was being totally honest. "He's a great guy. And I think he and your mom are much more compatible than the two of us ever were."

"Because of that whole head-hand thing?" Nick asked.

This was the excuse Mom and Dad gave for why their marriage hadn't worked out: Mom liked thinking; Dad liked doing. Mom could sit around all day talking about things that, as far as Nick was concerned, really didn't make any sense. Dad hated sitting around. His job was building houses, and even when he wasn't at work he was always making something: a garden or a pot of stew or a bookshelf for Eryn's room or . . . something.

Nick didn't think it was that weird that Mom and Dad hadn't stayed together. What he didn't understand was why they'd ever gotten married in the first place.

Dad's explanation was, "Love makes you do strange things, kids."

Mom's explanation was . . . Well, actually, Nick had never listened all the way through Mom's explanation. It was something about biology and psychology and lots of other things Nick mostly didn't care about.

But Michael was a professor of computer science. He thought about things all the time too—just more interesting things than Mom thought about.

"I guess Mom must think Eryn and I are more like you than like her and Michael," Nick said, trying to sound casual and offhanded and *not* like freaked-out Eryn. "Mom said we didn't have anything in common with Michael's kids. They must be too smart for us."

Will this work? Nick wondered.

Dad had started driving again when the light turned green, but now he hit the brake so hard that Nick's head jerked forward, and a car behind them honked its horn.

Dad yanked the steering wheel to the right, pulling over to the side of the road. The car shuddered to a stop.

Dad spun in his seat so he was facing Nick directly.

"Too smart for you? *Too smart for you*?" Dad repeated, his face turning redder and redder and his hair puffing out more than ever. "Don't you ever let me hear either one of you say *anybody* is too smart for the Stone twins. You hear me? You two are plenty smart. You're the perfect mix of your mother *and* me, so you're good with both your heads and your hands."

It's working, Nick thought.

"Yeah, but you have to say you think we're smart and talented and all, because you're our dad," Nick said with a shrug. "Those other kids must be geniuses or prodigies or something."

Dad's face was so red he looked like a tomato. But—this was weird—rather than going on shouting at Nick, Dad glanced cautiously out the window. They had pulled over right beside the park with the giant playground where Nick and Eryn had played when they were younger. Even though it was starting to get dark, there were still some moms and dads pushing little kids on swings or waiting at the bottom of the big curvy slides for their toddlers to come down.

The next time Dad spoke, it was in a much softer voice. Could he possibly be afraid someone would overhear him? Why?

It's not a crime to tell your kids they're smart, Nick thought.

"Michael's kids . . . they're just different," Dad said. "That's all. It doesn't mean anything bad about them or bad about you."

"Wow, that really clears things up," Eryn said sarcastically from the backseat. "So are you saying it's being different that's bad?"

Dad shook his head like Eryn had confused him.

"No, no, differences are *fine*," he said. "Differences aren't a problem at all. We need all sorts of different kinds of people in the world to make things work right. Like your mom and me. If there weren't people like me, nobody would have a house. And if there weren't people like your mom, kids wouldn't understand their feelings. So—"

"So it's just kids who are different who shouldn't have anything to do with each other?" Eryn asked. "Kids like Ava and Jackson and Nick and me?"

Dad ran his hand through his hair. Now it wasn't just curly and wild; it also stuck up in odd places.

"This is really more your mom's department than

mine," he muttered. "Look, your mom and Michael are just trying to make the transition easier for everyone. *You're* smart, good kids, and Ava and Jackson are smart, good kids, but you just can't meet. Not until . . ."

"Until what?" Eryn asked, springing forward like a cat pouncing. "You're saying the plan is for all of us to meet someday? When? Mom said we'd *never* have to meet those kids."

Nick turned around and glared at Eryn. Was she *trying* to get Dad to stop talking?

Dad looked lost.

"Um . . . maybe you should save your questions for your next phone call with Mom," he said. He winced. "Or really, until you see her next Sunday night. Because it's better to talk about difficult topics in person."

"Right, and you're the person we're with this week," Eryn argued. "That's why we're talking about it with you."

"I said, wait until Sunday!" Dad thundered.

Nick and Eryn sat in stunned silence. Dad *never* yelled at them like that. Dad never yelled at them; Mom never yelled at them; their teachers never yelled at them. . . .

Is this what it feels like? Nick wondered. *To be yelled at for something that isn't even your fault?*

Maybe he was like Mom: He could examine a feeling and label it and think that could make it easier to deal with.

Beside Nick, Dad clapped his hand over his mouth. Color drained from his face—in an instant it went from tomato red to ghostly pale. Dad put his other hand on the steering wheel, then down on the gearshift, then back on the steering wheel.

He dropped his hand from his mouth.

"I'm sorry, kids," he said, as meek as a mouse. "I guess I'm a little weirded out by all the changes too."

He put the car back in gear, and they drove the rest of the way home in silence.

"Want help carrying your things in?" Dad said as he pulled into the garage. His voice sounded like he was trying way too hard to make it come out normal.

"No thanks," Nick mumbled.

"We're fine," Eryn echoed.

It was strange that Dad was even asking. The only things they ever carried back and forth between their parents' houses were their backpacks for school. They didn't bother with suitcases. They just wore one set of clothes when they were at Dad's, and a different set of clothes when they were at Mom's. Nick's T-shirts and sweatshirts and jeans were all pretty interchangeable anyway, so it wasn't like he cared.

"We'll be upstairs in our rooms doing homework," Eryn said.

"Okay," Dad said, and this was weird too. Normally he would have asked what the homework was.

They went into the house, and Dad began dusting bookshelves that already looked completely dust-free. Nick followed Eryn upstairs. As soon as they got to the landing, Eryn grabbed Nick's arm and tugged him into her room with her.

She shoved the door shut behind them and whirled around to face Nick directly.

"Want to know what I heard Mom and Dad say?" she asked. "They were talking about risks! They said we're in danger, and so are those mystery kids of Michael's!"

Nick's heart pounded, and for a moment he wondered what it would feel like to faint, right there on Eryn's fluffy purple rug.

Then maybe the extra blood to his brain helped a little, and his mind cleared.

He sank down to sit on the edge of Eryn's bed.

"You know how Mom talks," he said. "I bet she meant *emotional* danger and *emotional* risks. That's all.

Remember when she had you thinking fourth grade was going to be a war zone, because she kept talking about landmines and 'battles unique to the female young of the human species'?" When really, all she meant was that some girls might make fun of other girls' clothes and hair?"

"This is different," Eryn said stubbornly. "Dad *yelled* at us."

Nick couldn't argue with that.

A knock sounded at Eryn's door.

"Can I come in?"

It was Dad. Eryn went over and yanked the door open.

Dad stood there panting a little, as if he'd raced up the stairs.

"I just wanted to tell you," he said. "At times like this, when there are a lot of changes going on, weird is normal. It's to be expected. So . . . don't think it's weird that we all feel weird. Everything that's going on right now is totally normal."

Eryn put her hands on her hips.

"Mom told you to say that," she accused.

Dad looked back and forth between Eryn and Nick.

"That doesn't mean it isn't true," he said.

But even he didn't sound like he believed it.

FIVE

Mom and Michael's new house had five bedrooms: one on the first floor for the two adults, and one each on the second floor for Eryn, Nick, Ava, and Jackson.

"Play it cool," Eryn whispered to Nick as they pulled up to the house in a U-Haul truck with their possessions from Mom's house boxed up in the back. "Don't act like the first thing you want to do is snoop on the other kids."

Nick shook his head and rolled his eyes at her, as if to say, *Duh! Do you think I'm an idiot?*

But Eryn knew: The first thing both of them wanted to do was to snoop on the other kids.

It'd been three months since Mom had announced she and Michael were getting married, and Eryn and Nick knew no more about Michael's kids than they had the first day. Mom and Michael had taken all the kids to see the new house before they made an offer on it—but Michael's kids had gone on a different day than Eryn and

Nick. Mom and Michael had gotten married on a cruise in the Caribbean and taken ten days for the honeymoon. This messed up the schedule of Eryn and Nick spending one week at Mom's and one week at Dad's—the very first time Eryn could remember that happening. Eryn thought the mess-up and the move could mean an overlap with Michael's kids at the new house, but when she hinted at a longer time at Mom's the next week, Dad had looked hurt.

"Eryn, we don't have to even things up," he said. "It's been great having you and Nick around for ten days, not just a week. I'd love to have you live with me all the time, if I could."

"Except the two of us always strive to be fair to everyone involved," Mom had finished for him. "And what's fair to the two of you—and Dad and me, and Michael and his kids—is to simply go back to our normal schedule, as usual."

So no overlap with Ava and Jackson, Eryn thought.

Now Mom parked the U-Haul, and Eryn shoved open the door and started racing for the house.

"Eryn—take a box with you!" Mom called off after her. "We're going to have to go back and forth enough times as it is, without you wasting trips!"

Eryn let out an exasperated snort and spun around. Michael had come out to the curb and already had the back of the truck open. He handed her a box.

"Glad you're so eager to get into the house," Michael said. "That's a good sign for our future as a family, isn't it?"

"I guess," Eryn said.

Michael was tall and bald and had a very narrow face—had Mom picked him because he looked the opposite of Dad? Did Mom think Michael was better-looking?

Eryn felt disloyal even thinking that.

She carried her box up the driveway, but had to wait while Michael unlocked the front door.

"Your bedroom's the first one on the right, up the stairs," Michael said.

If it had been Mom telling her that, Eryn might have argued, *What? We don't even get to choose our own rooms?* Or *Did you let* Michael's *kids choose first? That's not fair!* But since it was Michael, Eryn just said, "Okay."

Mom probably knew I wouldn't argue if Michael delivered the news, Eryn thought darkly. *She probably* planned *for him to be the one to tell us. I should tell Mom I know what she's up to, and argue with her anyway!*

But Eryn might be just one staircase away from finally learning something about the mysterious stepsiblings she'd been wondering about for months. She wasn't going to delay any more than she had to.

She walked through the living room, where the green sofas from Mom's house had been paired with orangey-tan end tables that must have come from Michael's condo—they looked odd together, but maybe that was just because Eryn wasn't used to the combination. She climbed the stairs and took her box into the first room on the right. It was slightly bigger than her old bedroom back at Mom's. Her furniture was already here too, and it looked just as out of place as the sofas downstairs. The bed was dwarfed by the huge window above it, and the desk looked lonely all by itself on the far wall.

What are you going to do—complain because you have too much space? Eryn wondered.

She put her cardboard box down on the floor and went back into the hall. Nick was just stepping into the room across from hers. She tapped him on the shoulder, then put her finger to her lips.

Nick nodded and put down the box he'd been holding. He had to be thinking just like her.

Together, they tiptoed toward the other end of the hall, where there were three more doors. The door in the middle was partly open, leading into a bathroom.

The other two doors were shut.

"Their rooms," Eryn whispered. She didn't even have to say *Ava's and Jackson's*.

Nick nodded again and reached for the doorknob on his side of the hallway.

How much can you find out about two kids just by seeing their bedrooms? Eryn wondered.

She thought about how her hyper-organized friend Megan had the books on her bookshelves arranged in alphabetical order like a library; she thought about how her craftsy friend Caitlyn always had a trail of glitter and paint scattered across the floor of her room.

Plenty, Eryn told herself.

She reached for the doorknob on her side of the hall and eagerly twisted it to the right.

The doorknob didn't turn.

"Are, like, the doorknobs in this house backwards or something?" she hissed to Nick, twisting her hand to the left instead.

But the doorknob didn't turn that way either.

Eryn rammed her shoulder against the top part of

the door. Nothing. She hit it again. The door still didn't budge.

Nick pulled her back from slamming into the door a third time.

"It's no use," he said. His eyes were wide and stunned. "The doors are locked. They've locked us out. Why would they do that?"

Eryn didn't have an answer.

SIX

"So, kids, how do you like the new house?" Michael asked at dinner that night. "Now that you've lived in it for all of six hours?"

"It makes me feel like Bluebeard's wife," Eryn said, pressing taco meat down into her taco so firmly that the shell cracked.

Dad would have made a joke about how he didn't know Eryn had a husband now; he would have moaned, *If you're old enough to get married, how old does that make me?*

Michael just blinked vacantly—maybe he'd picked up the blinking from Mom.

"I don't think I know that reference," he said cautiously. "Is it something from TV? A movie? A book?"

"Oh, Eryn, don't be so melodramatic," Mom said as she passed Nick a bowl of refried beans. She turned to Michael. "Bluebeard's wife is a character in a French fairy tale. Her husband gives her a key to a locked room, but tells her she's not allowed to open the door. She opens the door anyway, and she finds the dead bodies of her husband's previous wives."

Nick glanced down at the refried beans he'd been about to put on his plate. They didn't look very good to him right now. In fact, they kind of looked like guts that might have spilled out of a dead body. He put the bowl down on the table and raised an eyebrow at Eryn, shorthand for, *You really want to go there our first night in the new house?*

Eryn gave a tiny nod.

Nick thought about all the secretive strategies they'd tried that afternoon: going into the backyard and trying to peek in Ava's and Jackson's windows (no luck—they were covered by blinds); trying to slide a yardstick under the doors to feel around that way (the yardstick just got caught on the carpeting); trying to speculate on all sorts of possibilities while dodging Mom and Michael coming in and out with boxes.

This afternoon they'd been so worried about getting caught. Evidently Eryn didn't care about that anymore.

"Do you think there might be *dead bodies* in Ava's and Jackson's rooms?" Nick asked, helping out. "Because the doors are locked?"

Mom sighed. She picked up the bowl of refried beans and put a spoonful on Nick's plate.

"Even in the new house, you still have to eat a balanced meal," she said. She turned her head so she could talk to Eryn and Nick both at once. "The two of you are being ridiculous. This is *not* like the Bluebeard story, because you don't have the key to a door you're not supposed to unlock. And there aren't dead bodies here. Do you assume our neighbors have dead bodies in their houses just because they lock their front doors? The Bluebeard story is about patriarchal abuse of power and feminist subverting of that power. This is simply about being respectful of others' possessions. We'll lock your doors too, when Ava and Jackson are here. You wouldn't want them rooting around in your rooms either, would you?"

Nick was still stuck back on the words "patriarchal abuse of power and feminist subverting of that power." What did that even mean?

He decided it didn't matter. Was Eryn maybe blowing the whole locked-door situation out of proportion? Mom was right about one thing: He wouldn't like the idea of strange kids going into his bedroom when he was away at Dad's.

Then Mom turned to face Michael.

"I'm sorry Nick and Eryn are behaving like this," she said.

Nick narrowed his eyes. Why did Mom feel like she had to apologize for them? Was this what it was going to be like from now on, Mom always siding with Michael against Eryn and Nick?

Michael looked away from Mom, toward Nick. Eryn kicked Nick under the table. Nick knew that kick meant, *If Michael wants to make peace with some male bonding—like if he offers extra video game time after dinner—don't fall for it!*

"Hey," Michael said weakly. "Um . . ."

Maybe Michael's kids never argued with him or their mom. Maybe that's how they were different. Maybe they were always obedient little angels and Michael had no idea what he'd gotten into, marrying Mom and having Nick and Eryn as stepchildren.

Nick made sure his face didn't show any sympathy for Michael.

Michael took his napkin from his lap and placed it on the table beside his plate of mostly untouched tacos.

"I was going to save this as a surprise for later, but look what I programmed some of our picture frames to do," he said.

He stood up and went over to a pile of frames leaning against the living room wall, waiting to be hung. He picked up one of the frames and brought it back to the table. As he walked, he touched some control on the side of the frame, and instantly the picture inside the frame changed from a nature scene of autumn leaves to a pairing of Nick's and Eryn's sixth-grade school pictures. Even if Nick ever wanted to pretend he and Eryn weren't twins—or not related at all, maybe—these pictures would have prevented it. Both of them had the same dark-brown hair, though Eryn's flowed down to touch her shoulders and Nick kept his cut short (to avoid having it turn into the same kind of curly mess that grew on his dad's head). In the pictures, they both had the same open, trusting, friendly expression on their faces. There was probably a reason they were always the ones chosen to escort new kids around at school: They looked completely nonthreatening. They looked like even if somebody was hiding dead bodies in their house, they wouldn't suspect a thing.

Eryn was not wearing her school-picture expression now.

"Let me guess," she said sarcastically. "You programmed all the picture frames to switch from pictures of Nick and me one week to pictures of Ava and Jackson the next. And—we're never going to be able to see any of the pictures of Ava and Jackson!"

Michael tilted his head and peered back at her. He looked a little hurt.

"You have part of it right," he said. "But I was thinking we could switch out the pictures anytime we wanted. Or just have it set on an endless loop, to change every half hour or something like that. Because, of course, sure, it's fine for you to see Ava's and Jackson's pictures too. Look."

He touched the control on the side of the frame and there, at last, was Eryn and Nick's first view of Ava and Jackson.

Their pictures, anyway.

Ava and Jackson both looked to be roughly the same age as Nick and Eryn—maybe only eleven, maybe already thirteen, maybe exactly twelve. Jackson had sandy-brown hair and a little scar in his eyebrow that made him look slightly more mischievous than Nick. Ava's curly reddish hair was the same length as Eryn's, but that was nothing unusual—most girls Nick knew had pretty much the same length hair. Ava had a sweet smile, and she held her eyes so wide open that Nick guessed she never squinted suspiciously at anyone, the way Eryn did. Unlike Eryn, Ava probably wouldn't ever get permanent squint lines between her eyes.

"Are they twins too?" Eryn asked. "And are they the same age as us? Why didn't you tell us all that already?"

Mom touched something on the side of the frame that made the whole thing go blank.

"The more we tell you, the more you want to know," Mom said. "Really, Eryn, how much information is enough?"

Eryn squirmed in her seat.

"I don't know," she said. "You could just let us meet Ava and Jackson, and we could ask them questions directly. That would probably be enough."

"And I've told you that isn't going to happen," Mom said in a steely voice. "Subject closed. Nick, are you going to eat those beans or not?"

SEVEN

Eryn stood at the top of the staircase. Moonlight streamed in through the huge picture window at the front of the house, directly across from her. She glanced over her shoulder, back into the darkness where she knew the hallway ended near two locked doors.

She wished she'd never heard the story of Bluebeard and his wife. She wished she and Nick had never brought up the possibility of dead bodies.

Silly, you know it's nothing like that, she scolded herself. *You know Mom. You know she's not a serial killer. You know she wouldn't marry a serial killer.*

She could imagine the kind of joke Nick might make about that: *Yeah, Mom would never keep dead bodies lying around the house. She'd say it was unsanitary.*

Eryn noticed a thin band of light under Nick's door. He was still awake. She tapped quietly at his door.

"Come in," he called.

Eryn shoved the door open and stepped into Nick's room. In the past couple of hours he'd turned it into a familiar place. His lacrosse trophies were lined up on top of his dresser, along with the globe that Mom had bought him when he was five and he'd started telling everyone he was going to grow up to be a world-famous explorer. Eryn couldn't remember the last time he'd told someone he was going to be a world-famous explorer. (Good thing—twelve-year-olds got laughed at for statements like that.) But the globe had always sat on his dresser back at Mom's old house, and Eryn liked seeing it here, too.

Either Nick or, more likely, Mom, had made Nick's bed with his old familiar sports-themed comforter and sheets, with the random pictures of baseballs and basketballs and hockey pucks all over the place. Had Nick been in second or third grade when he got that bedding to replace the Lego-themed bedding he'd had before? Was it the same time that Eryn replaced her Disney Princess bedding with a comforter covered with hot-pink-and-purple flowers and stripes?

If I got into Ava's and Jackson's rooms and saw that they still had Lego or princess bedding, then would I know everything I needed to know about them? Eryn wondered.

She remembered Mom's question at the dinner

table: *Really, Eryn, how much information is enough?*

She didn't know the answer to that question.

"I saw a cleat mark on the carpet downstairs," Nick said, without turning around from lining up books on his bookshelf. "You haven't been walking around with cleats on, have you? Maybe it's a sign that Ava and Jackson play sports where they have to wear cleats."

"Maybe," Eryn said. She sat down on Nick's bed and watched him for a minute. He seemed to be arranging his books based on which sport the main characters in the books played. She could tell by the basketballs, baseballs, and soccer balls on the spines.

"At least now we've seen pictures of Ava and Jackson," Nick said.

"Yeah . . . ," Eryn said. She thought for a moment. "But didn't something about those pictures seem kind of weird?"

"They looked like normal kids to me," Nick said, finally turning around to look at her.

"That's the problem," Eryn said. "Didn't they look maybe too normal? Like those pictures you see in frames at stores where it's just some actors or models trying too hard to look like normal people?"

She expected Nick to give her one of his *You know*

you're crazy, don't you? looks. He bit his lip instead.

"You're right," he said slowly. "You're exactly right. That is what they reminded me of. I just didn't figure that out until you said it."

It made her feel better and worse, all at once, to have Nick agree with her.

"But what if Ava and Jackson would think the same thing, looking at our pictures?" Nick asked.

Eryn stood up.

"I'm going downstairs to look at those pictures again," she said. "Want to come? Maybe we'll notice something else without Mom and Michael watching us."

"Sure," Nick said.

The two of them crept out of Nick's room together, both of them tiptoeing. That was ridiculous—it wasn't like they would get in trouble for going downstairs. If they needed to, they could always say they wanted a drink of cold water from the refrigerator, or they'd heard a noise and they wanted to see what it was, or . . .

Eryn tripped on the bottom step.

Nick grabbed her arm at the same time she caught the railing. In the silent house, the sound of his hand colliding with her arm and her hand colliding with the bannister seemed like a double thunderclap.

Both kids froze.

"Guess I'm not used to the new house yet," Eryn whispered, which was the understatement of the year.

"Do you think they heard us?" Nick whispered back.

Eryn looked toward the door to Mom and Michael's bedroom. It stayed closed. One of the couches blocked her view of the bottom of the door, so she couldn't even tell if they had a light on or not.

She began tiptoeing toward Mom and Michael's door.

"I thought we were coming down to look at the pictures!" Nick hissed at her.

"I have to make sure it's safe!" Eryn hissed back.

She circled the couch and saw a triangle of light on the floor. So Mom and Michael were still up. She pressed her ear against the door. Maybe the walls and doors were thinner in this house than in Mom's old one, because Eryn could hear perfectly here, even without the drinking-glass trick. Mom and Michael had soft music playing, which had probably covered over the sound of Eryn tripping. And along with the music . . .

"—shouldn't have shown them those pictures," Mom was saying.

"They're bound to be curious," Michael's voice rumbled in response. "It's human nature."

"Yes, but I don't want to encourage them," Mom said. "We've got to stifle that curiosity."

Eryn reeled back from the door. Was this really *Mom* talking? She'd been all about encouraging curiosity their whole lives. She was the one who'd bought Nick the globe, so he could pick out new places to explore. She was the one who'd told Eryn about prime numbers when she was only in first grade, and had encouraged Eryn to figure out and put up lists of prime numbers on the wall in her room. (Okay, Eryn had been a pretty weird little kid too, just like Nick.)

Eryn recovered and pressed her ear harder against the door.

"The way I see it, we give them innocent little details here and there, and they'll lose interest," Michael said. "Because it will start seeming routine and boring. And then they won't find out everything else."

"Everything else"? Eryn thought. *There's an "everything else"?*

"I thought I was supposed to be the psychology expert," Mom said sharply. "You're supposed to be better with computers."

"We're supposed to be good together," Michael said in such a smarmy voice that Eryn recoiled from the door.

Ugh, ugh, ugh, she thought. *Is Michael flirting?*

She didn't want to listen to that.

She began tiptoeing away from the door, back toward Nick. He was bent over something caught in the carpet, glinting in the moonlight.

"Look!" he whispered. "It's a red hair! Want to bet it's Ava's?"

Eryn studied the single hair Nick picked up from the carpet.

"That's what Michael would call an innocent little detail," she told him. "It's not enough. We're not going to stop until we find out everything. Everything *else*."

EIGHT

Life went on.

Nick thought anyone watching him and Eryn would assume very little had changed for them. They were living half the time in a house six blocks away from Mom's old house; they had a new stepfather—so what?

Lacrosse and tennis season ended, and basketball season started for both kids. Eryn got a part in the school play, and Nick got picked as stage manager. They did math homework and social studies projects; language arts essays and science labs. Thanksgiving, Christmas, and New Year's Day all passed in a blur.

But underneath it all, both Nick and Eryn were watching and waiting. Besides the red hair Nick had found on the carpet, Eryn found other red hairs in the bathroom, along with some that looked much shorter and sandy brown.

Nick agreed with Eryn that hair color and length was

just an "innocent little detail." But it seemed to prove that the pictures of Ava and Jackson really were pictures of Ava and Jackson.

Nick found a pencil under the living room couch that had been sharpened down to about half its normal length, so that the only words left on it were *iddle school honor roll student*. He and Eryn agonized for the rest of the day about how if only they could see the first part of the pencil, they'd know what school Ava and Jackson went to. They even imagined somehow going from school to school, asking if anybody had lost a pencil. But then at dinner that night, Mom said, "Has anybody seen my favorite pencil?" So it turned out that the pencil was just from the school where Mom worked, in the next town over from Maywood.

Nick was so disappointed that he hassled Mom. "What are you doing using a pencil that's supposed to belong to some kid at Cedarcreek? Did you steal it? Really, Mom? Stealing from an honor roll student?"

Sometimes it could be funny to hear Mom tie herself in knots trying to explain that she'd done nothing wrong

But before Mom could reply, Michael interrupted, "That's enough, Nick. Stop baiting your mother."

The look he gave Nick was both stern and annoyed.

Okay, that didn't go well, Nick thought.

Michael didn't scold Nick or Eryn often, but what if

he'd just been holding off at the beginning of the marriage? What if having a stepdad just meant that now there were three adults who'd tell Nick off whenever he did something wrong?

Across the table Eryn wiggled her eyebrows up and down at Nick. Nick couldn't figure out what she meant. He gave her his best *If you can think of anything to help me out, go for it* look.

"Mom, Nick and I can do the dishes tonight, even though it's not our turn," she said. "That way, you and Michael can catch up on your work or read or watch TV, whatever you want."

"That's very nice, Eryn," Mom said. "Thank you."

"We accept your offer," Michael said, grinning.

That's supposed to help me? Nick wondered, glaring at Eryn. *Making yourself look good when I just got yelled at?*

Eryn motioned with her head for Nick to help her start clearing plates from the table. Nick picked up the spaghetti bowl and followed her into the kitchen.

"Thanks a lot," he muttered.

"I just got an idea, and I wanted to tell you as soon as possible," Eryn said. "This was the quickest way I could think of."

"Okay," Nick said.

Eryn rinsed off the one curl of spaghetti she'd left on

her plate and turned the garbage disposal on. Masked by its grinding roar, she told him, "We could just start calling schools and ask if Ava and Jackson go there. And then we could figure out a way to skip school someday and hang out at the other kids' school when they're coming out at the end of the day. We know what they look like. We could find them. We don't have to wait for Mom and Michael to give us permission to meet them."

Nick stared at his sister. This was far beyond asking questions and looking for hairs and cleat marks on the carpet. This was breaking rules. This was totally disobeying.

Nick thought about Michael glaring at him. He thought about how Michael was probably going to start scolding Nick and Eryn more and more. He thought about how much those locked doors at the back of the upstairs hallway bothered him every time he went past. He thought about how likely it was that he and Eryn would get caught if they skipped school.

But Mom and Michael wouldn't catch us until after *we met Ava and Jackson,* he thought. *Whatever punishment they'd choose, it'd still be worth it.*

"All right," he said. "Let's do it."

NINE

It was two forty-five p.m. School was out for the day, and Eryn was supposed to be in the auditorium in fifteen minutes to rehearse for the play. Rehearsal didn't involve changing clothes, so she thought this was a better day for sneaky behavior than one of the days when she had basketball.

Pretending she was only curious about how cloudy it looked outside, she walked away from all the other kids moving books into or out of their lockers and strolled toward the side door of the school. It looked cold and forbidding outside—the leafless January trees looked dead. Eryn held back a shiver and glanced at a list of numbers she and Nick had put together the night before. Then she punched one of those numbers into her cell phone.

"Bluffsview Middle School," a pleasant voice answered.

"Hi," Eryn said, trying to pull on the two days of

acting lessons she'd had for the school play. She tried to sound like a nice, respectable kid anyone would want to help.

Which, really, shouldn't feel so much like it required acting.

She swallowed hard and went on.

"I'm trying to find a friend who moved away a few years ago, and then I lost track of her," she said. This was the best story she and Nick had been able to come up with. "I know she's somewhere in Maywood, but I can't find her address or phone number. Do you have an Ava Lightner who goes there? Or maybe a Jackson Lightner? That's her brother."

"Oh dear, we can't give out personal information about our students," the woman said, sounding much more horrified than Eryn would have expected. "But I would like to help you. If you give me your name and contact information, I could put it out on the local school listserv, and maybe that could lead to your friend contacting you."

No, no, no, no, no! screamed in Eryn's brain. *I can't have my name on any school listserv! Mom would see it!*

She almost hung up or did the old *I'm sorry—I can't hear you. I think we've got a bad connection* trick. But what if the woman called Eryn back? What if she put Eryn's cell number on the listserv even without a name, because she wanted so badly to help?

"Oh, that's a great idea!" Eryn said, trying to sound grateful. "Except . . . oh darn, my parents get so worried about privacy and stuff like that. They wouldn't want my name and number—what would you call it? Publicized?"

"That is very sensible of your parents," the woman said approvingly.

"Right," Eryn said. "So, just as a favor, could you let me know anyway if Ava goes there?"

"No, I cannot," the woman said. "I'm sorry. Good-bye."

And then she hung up on Eryn.

Eryn stood there gulping in air, her heart pounding as if she'd just run all her warm-up laps at basketball practice. That had gone so much worse than she ever would have expected. It had gone so badly, she didn't dare try to call any of the other schools.

"Eryn, hurry up! You're going to be late!" her friend Caitlyn called behind her, from beside the lockers. "What are you doing over there?"

"Nothing," Eryn said quickly. "Just looking outside. Thinking."

"Oooh, that sounds dangerous," Caitlyn joked. "And you're really going to be in danger if you don't get into the auditorium right now. You know how Mr. Sondarelli gets upset if anyone's late."

Eryn turned and followed Caitlyn toward the auditorium. She laughed automatically at Caitlyn's teasing, but she didn't really listen as Caitlyn chattered on.

Caitlyn wore the most outlandish clothes of any of Eryn's friends—right now she had on army boots, a green-and-purple flowered peasant skirt, and an orange long-sleeved T-shirt. But that was the only radical thing about her. That was the only radical thing about any of Eryn's friends.

All of them would have been horrified if Eryn told them she had been thinking of skipping school to find Ava and Jackson. Eryn hadn't even told her friends anything about Ava and Jackson, because she knew they would think the whole thing was weird. It was weird enough that she had a new stepdad.

We're all such rule-followers, Eryn thought. *We go to school, we go to after-school activities, we go home and eat dinner and do our homework. It's like we're robots or something.*

It had taken the mystery of Ava and Jackson to make

her see how bland her life was, how ordinary and dull.

And I can't do *anything about it because there's no time with school and after-school activities and homework,* Eryn thought. *And Mom will find out and stop us if Nick and I try too hard to solve the mystery.*

She was stuck. And as far as she could tell, she and Nick would stay stuck and stymied on the Ava and Jackson mystery forever.

But everything changed that very afternoon: It started snowing.

TEN

"Two-hour delay!" Nick cried, stomping down the stairs. "Woo-hoo!"

He peered out the front window. From the midpoint of the staircase, all he could see outside was snow. Big, lazy flakes of it floated gently down from the sky.

"We don't have to be at school until ten!" he crowed.

"What? Where'd you hear that?" Mom said, looking up from the couch, where she was bent over her laptop.

"Ryan texted me," Nick said. Sometimes it paid to have a friend whose father was the school superintendent.

"But I haven't gotten any notification," Mom protested. She typed something on her keyboard. "Oh. Oh no. Maywood has the delay, but my school doesn't."

She abruptly got up and went into her bedroom. Nick could hear voices murmuring. Then she came back.

"No worries," she said. "Michael has an important meeting he can't miss at nine thirty, but he'll stay home with you and Eryn until then. So you'll only have a little time on your own before the bus comes."

Nick's excitement over the delay diminished a little.

"Mom, we're *twelve,*" he said. "We're old enough to stay home by ourselves for the whole two hours."

Mom seemed to be studying him a little too carefully.

"I wonder . . . ," she began.

"What?" Nick said.

"Well, Eryn seemed so moody last night, and now you're grumpy too—are both of you entering the brunt of the trials and tribulations of puberty?" she asked.

Nick knew why Eryn had been moody the night before: Her plan for finding Ava and Jackson had failed. Nick figured they'd just think of a different plan. But it wasn't as if he could tell Mom that.

And hearing Mom talk about puberty was about the last thing he wanted to do with his precious two-hour delay.

"How about we pretend you didn't just say that, and I'll go let Eryn know about the delay?" Nick offered.

"Nicholas!" Mom exclaimed. "Show some respect!"

Nick realized that if he wasn't careful, he could end up spending his whole two-hour delay confined to his room. Without electronics.

"Sorry, Mom," he said. "It was a joke."

"Young man, you need to understand that some jokes just aren't funny, and . . ."

Nick tuned Mom out and hoped that simply nodding as he walked up to Eryn's room would work. He tapped on Eryn's door.

"Come in," Eryn said groggily.

She was still in bed, even though she should already be downstairs getting her breakfast by now.

"We've got a two-hour delay because of the snow, but Mom doesn't," Nick said.

Eryn's face lit up.

"Two hours by ourselves?" she said. "We could—"

"Michael's staying home with us," Nick added.

Eryn's face fell.

"Oh," she said, and turned over as if she was just going back to sleep.

Nick looked around, and noticed that sometime last night Eryn had taken down most of the posters from her walls: the cute puppy and kitten posters with inspirational sayings, the five different views of Liam from The Best Band. A full band poster of TBB was torn in half by the trash can.

Yikes, Nick thought. *What was it Mom said Eryn*

might be starting? "The brunt of the worst trials and tribulations of puberty?"

He took a step backward, out of Eryn's room.

After Mom left for work, Michael let Nick play an hour of video games while Michael took care of some work e-mail. Eryn stayed in her room. At nine, Michael looked out at the snow—which seemed to be getting heavier—and said, "Kiddo, I think I'm going to need to take off now, to make it to my meeting on time. Your bus comes at nine forty-five. You and Eryn can make absolutely certain you don't miss that bus, right?"

"Sure," Nick said.

"You know your mother and I will consider this a test to see if you can be trusted to stay home on your own for even longer periods of time, don't you?" Michael said.

Why did adults always have to ruin good news with comments like that?

Michael left, and Eryn came downstairs.

"We have forty-five minutes to ourselves?" she said. "Do you think that's enough time to—?"

The phone rang just then. Nick picked it up. It was Mom.

"Maywood just canceled all classes today completely!" she said.

"Yes! Yes! Yes!" Nick screamed, pumping his fist up and down with every *Yes!*

Across the room, Eryn mouthed the words *Snow day?* Nick grinned and nodded. Eryn tilted her head thoughtfully, then crept toward him, like she wanted to eavesdrop. Or argue with Mom.

Nick turned to the side so Eryn couldn't grab the phone from his hand.

"No, Nick, this is awful." Mom's voice on the other end of the line sounded grim. "The snow is worse than ever. Michael's going to have to change his meeting—"

"He just left," Nick said.

"Oh, okay, I'll try to catch him on his cell," Mom said. "Don't go anywhere. I'll call right back."

"Where does Mom think we might go?" Eryn asked sarcastically as Nick hung up. Evidently she'd heard that part.

"Outside, I guess," Nick said, shrugging. "To build snowmen, or have a snowball fight, or something like that. Want to do that later on?"

He looked out the window. The wind had picked up, and now there was so much snow swirling around, it was hard to see even the mailbox at the end of the driveway.

"It's like something you'd read about in a book," Eryn said. "Where there's a blizzard and the pioneers have to hold a rope going out to the barn to milk the cows, or else they'll get lost and wander out onto the open prairie. . . ."

Why did she sound almost like she wanted to get lost wandering on the open prairie?

"Maybe we should wait until it calms down a little before we build our snowman," Nick said.

The phone rang again.

"Is Eryn there with you right now?" Mom asked when Nick picked it up. "Put me on speaker phone, so both of you can hear me at once."

"Okay," Nick said.

He pushed the speaker button and put the phone down on the table between him and Eryn.

"Michael's stuck in a snowdrift at the college," Mom said. "He's fine, but AAA told him it will be a few hours before they can get a tow truck out to him. Also, the city just closed down Apple Tree Boulevard because of an accident."

Apple Tree Boulevard was the only street leading from their neighborhood to either Mom's school or the college where Michael taught.

So neither Mom nor Michael can get home right now? Nick thought.

"And Dad's out of town at that builders convention, or else I'm sure you'd have him snowshoe over to take care of us," Eryn said, putting a bitter spin on her words.

Nick glared at her. What if she ruined everything by sassing Mom?

"I've tried the Chans, the Rodriguezes, and the Anthonys, but all of them left for work this morning before the worst of the storm hit," Mom said, naming the neighbors they knew best. "If we were still in our old neighborhood—"

"Mom, really, Eryn and I are fine on our own," Nick said quickly. "We are."

He narrowed his eyes at Eryn, hoping she'd get the message: *Don't mess this up!*

Apparently it worked, because Eryn shifted immediately from sullen, surly kid to Mommy's little angel.

"You know Nick and I are good at watching out for each other," Eryn said. "I'll make sure he doesn't go outside."

"I'll make sure Eryn doesn't make any messes," Nick added quickly, sticking his tongue out at Eryn. It was a good thing Mom couldn't actually see him.

Mom sighed.

"I don't think we have much choice," she said. "Things are supposed to clear up by midafternoon, so it shouldn't be more than three or four more hours that you're home alone. No more video games, Nick, because I know you already played some this morning. And I expect *both* of you to clean up after yourselves. And don't go outside *at all.* And—"

"We're on top of it, Mom," Eryn said, still with a saintly tone. Right now, she didn't sound like she even knew what sarcasm was. "We'll follow every single one of those rules."

"All right," Mom said reluctantly. "Call me if anything happens, anything at all . . ."

It took another ten minutes of them reassuring Mom before she finally hung up.

"Boy, she really knows how to ruin any possible fun," Nick grumbled. He sneaked a glance at Eryn. Would she really tattle on him if he spent the next few hours playing video games?

Eryn's face was lit up like a lightbulb. Nick wasn't sure he'd ever seen her look so excited.

"I can't believe she didn't make us promise not to do the one thing I'm dying to do," Eryn said.

"What?" Nick said blankly, squinting at her.

Eryn reached into her jeans pocket and pulled out something small and thin and black. It looked like one of those metal things girls put in their hair if some strands weren't quite long enough to be pulled back in a ponytail.

A bobby pin. That's what it was called.

"We have a snow day and we're all by ourselves and you want to play with your *hair*?" Nick asked incredulously.

"No, stupid," Eryn said. "I want to pick the locks on Ava's and Jackson's rooms."

ELEVEN

We're doing this, Eryn thought, poking one end of the bobby pin into the hole in the center of Ava's doorknob. *We really are.*

She'd decided last night that their next step would have to be breaking in to Ava's and Jackson's rooms, but she hadn't been sure she and Nick would actually have the nerve. And when would they ever get the chance to do it? At night, when any noise could bring Mom or Michael up to investigate?

The snow was like a sign; Michael's car being stuck in the snowbank and Mom being stranded at school was like a gentle shove, accompanied by some voice only Eryn could hear: *You have to do this.*

"What if that pin gets stuck in the door?" Nick asked, hovering nervously behind her. "What if that makes Mom and Michael find out what you've done?"

"What *we've* done," Eryn corrected him. "It's not going to get stuck."

Right now she was more concerned that the lock was fortified somehow and the pin wouldn't work. But even without looking at Nick, she could feel him worrying behind her.

"If it does get stuck, I'll use the wire cutters on it, so Mom and Michael won't know what happened," Eryn added, to calm Nick down.

The pin hit something solid, directly behind the hole in the knob. Eryn pushed the pin harder. Something clicked.

"Is that . . . Did it work?" Nick asked.

Eryn pulled the bobby pin out of the hole and put her hand on the knob. She turned it and pushed tentatively on the door. It slid back a quarter-inch and came to rest at the very edge of the door frame. Another push would give her her first glimpse of Ava's room.

Eryn took a deep breath.

"Yes!" Nick began chanting behind her. "Yes, yes, yes. . . . Why'd you have to do the girl's room first?"

Eryn handed him the bobby pin.

"Right," Nick said. "We could do this almost like a ceremony. You step into Ava's room at the same time I step into Jackson's. We find out what we need to know at the exact same time. . . ."

"Less talking, more lock picking," Eryn said, waving him toward Jackson's door.

She wasn't sure how much longer she could wait before just shoving her way into Ava's room. What would it look like? How strange would someone have to be to have absolutely nothing in common with Eryn?

Nick bent in front of Jackson's door and maneuvered the pin into the lock.

"It goes straight in and then you have to push on it until it clicks," Eryn told him.

The click came just as Eryn was saying the word *click*.

"Now," Nick said. He turned the knob, pushed the door open, and stepped into Jackson's room. Eryn, scrambling to catch up, shoved Ava's door open all the way. It swung back and banged against the wall, knocking over a tennis racket.

A tennis racket? Eryn thought. *Just like mine?*

Ava's room was painted the same light turquoise as Eryn's room back at Dad's house. The first poster Eryn noticed was of Liam from The Best Band—almost exactly the same poster that had hung in Eryn's room until last night. A book of piano music lay on the desk.

It looks like she's a lot *like me,* Eryn thought numbly.

Maybe . . . maybe it's really just Jackson who's totally different from us?

But just as she thought that, she heard Nick scream from down the hall.

"No way! Eryn, you've got to see this! It's like Jackson cloned my room!"

TWELVE

Nick had been kind of braced for seeing dead bodies.

But what he saw struck him as even stranger: a lacrosse stick and a basketball spilling out of Jackson's closet, a trumpet mouthpiece balanced on the desk, a freaking *map* on the wall that might as well have been his own globe ironed out flat. Jackson even had the same sports books lined up on his bookshelf, with all the soccer balls, basketballs, and baseballs on the spines grouped together.

Nick could wake up in this room and barely notice any difference from his own.

He took a step out of Jackson's room and raced down the hall toward Ava's.

"What's it like in there?" he called to Eryn. "Oh."

Ava's room was like a combination of Eryn's room at Dad's, plus the way her room at Mom's had looked until last night. The Best Band posters were everywhere, and it looked like Liam was also Ava's favorite TBB member. A poster of an intense-looking girl playing tennis hung over the bed, with the word *Perseverance* in large letters at the bottom.

"Maybe we misunderstood?" Nick suggested. "Maybe Mom said Ava and Jackson are too *much* like us, and that's why they didn't want us to meet?"

"That's crazy," Eryn said. "And—that's not what she said."

She stood on the rug in the middle of Ava's room—the rug was striped, just like the one in Eryn's room. She slowly spun around, like she was trying to get her eyes to believe what she was seeing.

"Maybe . . . ," Eryn said, "maybe it's that Ava and Jackson are a lot like us in the activities they're involved in, but they have a bad attitude or something. So Mom and Michael are afraid that if we met them, their bad attitudes would rub off on us."

"You're the one with ripped-up posters in your trash can," Nick said.

"I don't have a bad attitude!" Eryn protested.

Nick decided not to say *Then why'd you tear up your posters?*

"Anyway, it was a long time ago that Mom and Michael

said we couldn't meet those other kids," Eryn said. "Back when I still had all these same kinds of posters on my wall."

She gestured at Ava's walls.

"How much do posters and bedspreads and tennis rackets tell you about what a person's like?" Nick asked.

"People change," Eryn said fiercely. "Kids outgrow things."

Nick guessed that was her answer to the question he hadn't asked, about why she'd ripped down and torn up her posters.

"We need to become, like, super-detectives or something," Nick said. "Find out what in these rooms really means anything."

Eryn walked over to the desk and began opening drawers.

"If we're lucky, Ava and Jackson keep journals, and they have separate ones for here and at their mom's," she muttered.

"Yeah, right," Nick said. "Anything like that, they'd keep on their laptops, and I'm sure they carry their laptops back and forth between their parents' houses. Just like we do."

There wasn't a laptop sitting on Ava's desk. Nick was pretty sure he would have noticed if there'd been one in Jackson's room.

All the same, he went over and peeked into the drawer Eryn had just opened. Pencils, pens, paper clips, and Post-it notes lay in a compartmentalized plastic container.

"She's neater than you," Nick observed. "Everything's perfect."

"Or it's fake," Eryn said, scowling. "Mom and Michael *want* us to think she's perfect."

"Mom and Michael didn't want us to be in this room, so why would they fake anything about it?" Nick asked.

Eryn turned her head toward Nick, but her eyes didn't really focus. She squinted even more fiercely than usual. Then she shook her head as if that might help her think straight.

"Or Ava is trying to act perfect for Mom and Michael," Eryn suggested. "This whole situation is crazy. Don't you feel it? Doesn't it seem like nothing in this room is *real*? Like it's all . . . staged?"

Like how the pictures of Ava and Jackson look like the fake photos put in frames for sale? Nick thought.

"And don't our rooms back at Dad's look 'staged' right now because we're not living there this week?" Nick asked. "Don't we always leave our rooms neater when we're going to be gone for the week than we do when we walk out every morning just to go to school?"

He found himself warming to the topic. He had a whole two weeks of experience as a stage manager—he knew about this.

"And think about how Mom always makes us clean up our rooms before we have friends over," he said. "Are you saying that looks staged too?"

Eryn stubbornly pursed her lips.

"This is different," she said. "There's nothing here that's personal."

Nick yanked open the drawer below the one with the pens and pencils. A manila envelope lay on the very top. It was facedown, but Nick could see the smear of a postal mark on the back.

"Look, a letter," he said. "Letters are personal."

Eryn picked the envelope up, flipped open the flap at the top, and let the envelope fall as she pulled out two flat sheets of paper. One seemed to be some sort of heavy embossed certificate. Eryn began reading aloud from the other.

"'Dear Ava, Thank you for your participation in our production of *The Ugly Duckling.* We appreciate the dedication of all our actors and actresses . . .' Nick, this is just a form letter and a stupid certificate," Eryn moaned. "And it just proves that she had a role in a play. Like me."

"Does it have the name of her school?" Nick asked. "That would be something."

He bent over to pick up the manila envelope Eryn had dropped.

"No, it's from some community theater," Eryn said. "So she and Jackson could be at any school around here."

Nick saw the words *Maywood Children's Community Theater*, on the return address of the envelope just as Eryn said that. Eryn was still talking—something about how maybe she and Nick could get Mom and Dad to let them try out for the community theater, as a way to get to Ava and Jackson. But no, Mom and Dad would probably say no to that and just not say why, because . . .

Nick stopped listening to Eryn. Instead he started tapping her on the arm to get her to stop talking. Because he'd found something even more important.

"Eryn, Eryn—shut up and *look*," he said, waving the front of the envelope in front of her.

"Why—what?" she asked.

"This wasn't mailed to Ava at this house," Nick said. He pointed to the address in the center of the envelope. "So this must be the address for Ava and Jackson's mom. What do you want to bet they're having a snow day too? So we could go and meet them *right now*?"

THIRTEEN

The words swam before Eryn's eyes: "4083 Briarthorn Lane, Maywood, Ohio." She didn't know where Briarthorn Lane was. But if it was close, could she and Nick actually go there? Could it be that Ava and Jackson were home alone right now too?

She imagined trekking through the snow, knocking at a strange door, and then . . . what? What would she have to say to Ava and Jackson?

She remembered that she and Nick had promised Mom they wouldn't go outside.

"I'll go look up that address," Nick said, scurrying out of the room.

Eryn let him go. For a moment she just stood there staring at walls painted her favorite color. Then she called after her brother, "Make sure you do it on your computer or mine. Don't use Mom's computer downstairs. Don't do anything she or Michael could trace."

"Why would I go all the way downstairs?" Nick called back. A moment later she heard him cry out, "Oooh . . ."

Eryn turned and raced after him. She found him in his room, staring at his laptop screen.

"It's three miles away," Nick said. "I bet it's closer if we walk through Lipman Park instead of going around it."

He pointed to the map he'd pulled up on the screen. Lipman Park, which was right in the center of Maywood, was a huge oval of green. Nick was right—it would probably be less than a mile if they went through the park.

Eryn looked out Nick's window. The snow was still coming down heavily.

"If we're already disobeying by breaking in to Ava's and Jackson's rooms, what difference does it make if we break Mom's rule about going outside, too?" Nick asked, as if he could tell she'd been thinking about that.

Um, because going out in a blizzard could get us killed? Eryn thought, but didn't say. She knew there wasn't actually a blizzard outside. It just looked like one.

She fiddled with the edge of Nick's laptop, where the protective case was coming loose.

"Doesn't breaking a direct promise seem worse?" she asked.

She thought about how weird she'd felt last night,

when she'd walked into her room and everything about it had seemed wrong. The perfect faces of Liam and the other members of The Best Band had suddenly seemed annoying, instead of dreamy like they always had before. The cheery kitten and puppy posters had seemed cloying and stupid, not cute.

Evidently she was the kind of girl who could suddenly start hating things she used to love. The kind of girl who would rip up posters. The kind of girl who would break into her stepsiblings' rooms. Did that mean she was also the kind of girl who would make a deep, serious, heartfelt promise to her mother—and then turn around and break it barely forty-five minutes later?

But how could they *not* go try to find Ava and Jackson now, while they had the chance?

"You just think it seems worse because we're more likely to get caught this way," Nick argued. "Ava and Jackson's mom might see us. And unless we get a lot more wind and snow at exactly the right time, Mom and Michael would see our footsteps in the snow . . ."

"Yeah, they would," Eryn said hopelessly.

Wasn't there any way this could still work?

Suddenly Eryn saw a way to do it. She yanked her cell phone out of her back pocket. She noticed that her friends had sent her six text messages, but she ignored them all and called Mom.

"What's wrong?" Mom said, by way of a greeting.

"Nothing's wrong," Eryn said soothingly. "Nick and I are fine." She was even careful to say *Nick and I* instead of *me and Nick*. "I was just thinking, there's already a lot of snow in the driveway. You and Michael are going to have trouble getting into the garage when you get home.

"I know you wanted us to stay inside, but if the snow slows down a little, would it be okay if we went out to shovel off the driveway for you? We'll be careful. We'll stick together, so both of us are safe."

The phone was silent for a moment. Then Mom said, "Eryn, that is very mature of you to think that way. *If* the snow slows down, and *if* you are careful, then yes, you can go outside. But promise you'll stay in our yard and driveway."

Eryn frowned. That didn't help!

She noticed that Nick had leaned his head close, so he could hear Mom's answer. Now he put his hand on the phone, turned it toward his mouth, and spoke into it. "Oh. I was thinking if we had time maybe we'd shovel Mr. Cohen's sidewalk and driveway too. Since, you know, he's so old, he probably can't do it himself."

Nick grinned at Eryn. Eryn held her breath. Would Mom fall for that?

Mom seemed to be thinking.

"Sometimes you two really do amaze me," she said. "Yes, if you want to shovel for Mr. Cohen, I have no problem with the two of you going around the corner. I'm proud of you for being so considerate. But *do* be careful, and promise you *will* stick together."

"Like glue," Eryn agreed.

"Superglue," Nick corrected, waggling his eyebrows triumphantly up and down at Eryn.

As soon as they hung up, Nick punched Eryn in the arm.

"Genius, right?" Nick asked, grinning.

"You could have picked a neighbor with a shorter driveway," Eryn said, even as she grinned back at him. She looked at her watch and her smile faded a little. "We're going to have to work fast. First we need to go through Ava's and Jackson's rooms and see if there's anything else of interest. Then we need to make sure we put everything back exactly the way we found it, so no one can tell we were in there. Then we need to do all that shoveling. Then—"

"Then we need to go around a lot of corners," Nick said. "All the way to Briarthorn Lane."

FOURTEEN

They were lucky: The snow was the dry, powdery kind that shoveled easily. A lot of it blew back onto the driveway as soon as they dumped it into the yard, but Nick and Eryn weren't really trying to clear the pavement. They were just making it look like they'd tried.

"That's good enough," Eryn said as Nick got down to the end of the driveway and emptied his last shovelful. Her voice was muffled by the scarf wrapped around her head.

"Should we do Mr. Cohen's driveway now or later?" Nick asked. "First thing or afterwards?"

He could tell Eryn was struggling with the answer.

"Now, I guess," she said reluctantly.

They tramped down the block and turned onto Oriole Drive. All the streets in their new neighborhood were named for birds. Nick hadn't taken the time to look closely, but apparently all the streets in Ava and Jackson's mom's neighborhood were named for plants, or parts of plants.

Nick hoisted his shovel over his shoulder and felt a folded-up piece of paper rustle inside his coat. It was the map they'd printed out for getting to Briarthorn Lane. Eryn had insisted on it.

"We'll have our phones with us," Nick had argued, trying to cut down on the number of tasks they had to do before leaving the house.

"Right, and we need to turn off the GPS function on the phones so Mom can't tell where we go," Eryn argued. "I'm pretty sure that means we can't use Wi-Fi."

Nick was kind of amazed that Eryn would think of something like that. That was spy stuff. She was a twelve-year-old wearing pink snow boots. Nick couldn't make the two things fit together in his mind.

Mom and Michael wouldn't really try to track us on GPS—would they? Nick wondered. *Don't they trust us?*

Why should Mom and Michael trust them when Nick and Eryn were doing things Mom and Michael didn't want them to do?

Nick knew that getting permission to go "around the corner" didn't really make it right.

Just go find out why Mom and Michael don't want us meeting Ava and Jackson, Nick told himself. *Then worry about the consequences.*

They got to Mr. Cohen's house, and Eryn began pushing her shovel ahead of her on the sidewalk, making a path.

"You go up to his house and let him know we're here," she told Nick. "So we have an alibi. And a witness."

Was Eryn maybe a little too good at thinking like a criminal?

Nick copied her technique with his shovel, clearing a path to Mr. Cohen's front door. The snow swirled around him as he stood on Mr. Cohen's front porch and rang the doorbell. From inside the house, Nick could hear a TV turned up loud, some talk show–type yammering about politics and "the type of world we're going to leave for our children."

Nobody came, so Nick gave up on the doorbell and pounded his fist against the front door. He took off his glove so the pounding wouldn't be so muffled.

Finally Mr. Cohen opened the door a crack. Nick could see that the old man was wearing sweatpants under a thick terrycloth robe.

"Hi," Nick said. "We're the Stone kids from around the corner. We're shoveling off your driveway and sidewalk so you can get out if you want."

"Wasn't planning to," Mr. Cohen grunted. He stood there blankly for a moment. His sparse hair was matted on one side of his head, like he hadn't even bothered combing it yet this morning. "But—thanks. Um . . . you weren't expecting me to pay, were you?"

"No, no," Nick said, trying to sound generous and kind. "It's our gift to you."

"Oh," Mr. Cohen said. "Okay. That's good. I'm on a fixed income, you know."

He shut the door in Nick's face. Nick went back to Eryn, who'd already started on the driveway.

"Don't work too hard," Nick told her. "He doesn't care if we shovel or not."

"Alibi," Eryn said, panting a little as she tossed a shovelful to the side. "Witness. Plausible deniability."

Where did she come up with this stuff?

"He's going to remember what time we were here," Nick warned, digging his shovel into the next swath of untouched snow. "He'll remember which TV show he had on."

"He's a confused old man," Eryn said. "We can say he's wrong about the time, just right that we were here. And the driveway will prove it."

"Not if it's snowed over again," Nick muttered.

"Then we can stop on our way back and freshen things up," Eryn said calmly.

They were done in under fifteen minutes.

They considered stashing the shovels somewhere, because they could walk faster without them, but Eryn decided they needed the cover story of being kids out looking to make some money in the snowstorm. They both balanced the shovels against their shoulders and took off toward Lipman Park: Oriole to Raven to Eagle's Wing, and then into the neighborhood where all the streets were mammalian: Lion's Paw Drive to Elephant Street to Wolf's Howl Parkway. . . .

"Why do you think we didn't find anything else interesting in Ava's and Jackson's rooms?" Eryn asked as they slipped and slid along unshoveled sidewalks. Evidently everyone else was waiting until the snow stopped before attacking the drifts.

"Maybe Ava and Jackson just aren't very interesting kids," Nick suggested. "Maybe the real problem is that they're totally boring, and that's what Mom and Michael don't want us to find out."

"Nobody's totally boring," Eryn countered. "People are fascinating."

This was one of Mom's lines, something she'd used on them when they were younger and complained about not liking certain kids in their class.

They'd quickly learned not to complain about anyone. Even the boy who still picked his nose every day of third grade. Even the girl whose favorite topic for every conversation was ear wax.

"Mr. Cohen is boring," Nick said. "He just stood there like, *duuhhh* . . ."

Nick did an open-mouthed imitation that would have included drool if he hadn't been afraid it would freeze on his chin.

"One should always be compassionate toward the elderly," Eryn said loftily, imitating Mom again. "One could even argue that they are reminders to us that any one of us might someday face a battle against infirmities and disabilities and mental decline."

Nick snorted.

"You're mean," he said.

"Me?" Eryn protested. "You're the one making fun of a defenseless old man!"

They struggled onward through the snowdrifts for a few moments in silence. The wind seemed fiercer than ever, cutting in under the hood of Nick's coat.

"Do you really think I'm mean?" Eryn asked. "Is that my true identity? Is that what Ava and Jackson might think of me?"

How was Nick supposed to answer that?

"Mom says you're not supposed to worry about what other people think of you," he said. "The question is, what are we going to think of Ava and Jackson?"

"No, the question is, what's the big secret about them?" Eryn asked. She stamped her foot hard, smashing a pile of fluffy snow completely flat. "And why are Mom and Michael trying so hard to keep us from finding it?"

FIFTEEN

Lipman Park, when they reached it, was a vast, frozen wasteland of drifted snow. Eryn's feet had been numb since back at Mr. Cohen's, and she couldn't understand how she could feel so cold even as she was sweating beneath her coat, sweater, and Under Armour.

Getting to the other side of Lipman Park seemed about as practical as walking across Siberia. Or to the South Pole.

Nick took the first step off the sidewalk, into the untouched terrain. He pulled his shovel down from his shoulder and planted the handle in the snow, like a flag.

"I claim this territory for Nicholas the First of Maywoodia!" he cried out.

Eryn quickly landed the handle end of her shovel beside his.

"And Eryn the First of Maywoodia!" she added.

She liked that he didn't even bother arguing,

Nunh-uh! I claimed it first! And she liked that neither one had looked around first to see if anyone was watching them. Not that anyone sane would be out in this weather *to* watch them.

I bet Ava and Jackson would never pretend snow shovels are flagpoles, she thought as she and Nick picked up their shovels again.

How could she think that when nothing in Ava's or Jackson's rooms had seemed much different from anything in Eryn's or Nick's rooms?

Was there the slightest detail about the other kids' rooms that had been different?

She trudged forward, directly into the wind, for several painful steps before the answer came to her. The difference wasn't something that had been in the other kids' rooms—it was something missing.

"Nick, hey, Nick," she said, pounding on his back. "Did you see any worthless treasures in Jackson's or Ava's rooms?"

Because she had her scarf over her mouth, the question came out more like, *Id oo ee a-ee orth-ss* . . .

She pulled the scarf back, and the snow that had piled up on it collapsed in on her neck. She shook it off and asked her question again.

Nick squinted back at her from beneath his ice-encrusted hood. He even had ice in the hair that poked out from underneath his knit cap.

"Worthless treasures?" he repeated.

"You know, like that feather you've had since you were five, because you said it gave you luck in a T-ball game," Eryn said. "Or the stone I picked up on that one picnic with Dad years ago—the one that looks like it has a ribbon of gold in it, even though everyone told me it isn't gold. The things Mom always says are pointless to keep, and why don't we just let her throw them out? But we never do."

"Maybe Ava and Jackson actually listen to her," Nick said. "Or Michael told them what she's like, and so they keep all their worthless treasures at their mom's."

"Maybe," Eryn said. She couldn't let go of the sense that she'd figured out something important—a major clue. She just didn't know why it would be important.

They kept walking through the deep snow. Eryn tried to avoid the drifts that were high enough to spill over into her boots, but it was hard to tell when everything around her was white and frozen. Even the air felt frozen.

"I put the posters back up in your room," Nick said as they passed the tree that stood in the middle of the park.

"You did? Why?" Eryn asked.

"I didn't want Mom or Michael to have any reason to

be suspicious about anything," Nick said. "We can't let them see that anything's changed."

Eryn guessed that he'd done that while she was still looking through Ava's and Jackson's rooms and he'd given up. It kind of seemed like she should be mad at him for messing with her posters without asking, but she felt grateful instead.

"Okay," she said.

They reached the far side of Lipman Park. Eryn liked knowing she was back on paved sidewalk, no matter how icy and slick it was. Briarthorn Lane was only a few blocks away now.

"You aren't thinking we'd knock on the door first thing, are you?" Nick asked. "I think we should scout around first and see if their mom or stepdad are home. Do they have a stepdad?"

"I don't know," Eryn said, and it bothered her that she didn't even know that. She shivered, and it wasn't just because of the snow melting against her neck.

She rewrapped her scarf and kept going.

Briarthorn Lane, when they reached it, looked a lot like their own street: pleasant two-story houses; a tree or two in every yard; everything muffled and still, as if the blanket of snow absorbed every motion and sound.

Eryn found herself wanting to tiptoe, which was almost impossible to do in snow boots. She started wishing her winter coat was white or cream-colored instead of bright purple. Any color that wouldn't stand out against all the snow.

"Forty sixty-seven . . . forty seventy-five . . . forty eighty-three," Nick whispered, coming to a stop in front of a Cape Cod–style house painted gray with blue trim.

Eryn felt a tremor of panic in her stomach.

"Don't just stand there!" she complained. "Don't be so obvious!"

"Is there a nonchalant way to spy on your secret stepsiblings?" Nick asked.

Eryn looked around. Of course nobody else was out in this weather. Pretending she was only trying to shield her face from the wind, she pulled her scarf tighter, bent her head down, and took off running toward an evergreen tree planted at the side of the house. As soon as she reached it, she dove down under the low branches.

The branches shook, dumping snow on her and, a moment later, Nick.

Good, she told herself. *It'll be like camouflage.*

She lifted her head, inched slightly closer to the house, and peeked in the nearest window.

SIXTEEN

"Let me see too," Nick hissed, coming up behind Eryn.

She turned her head just enough to frown at him, but scooted slightly to the left.

Eryn's shovel was in his way, so he took it from her and tucked it—and his own—under the tree branches, mostly out of sight. Then he pressed his forehead against the cold bottom pane of the window, his face just high enough to bring his eyes level with the lowest part of the glass. He could see a living room—or maybe it was a family room—with floral couches and ruffled curtains. He felt sorry for Jackson, and maybe for Ava, too; apparently their mom liked stupid fussy, frilly stuff.

Then Nick realized Ava and Jackson were sitting on one of the couches.

Why did it take me so long to notice them? Nick wondered.

How had they blended in so completely with the flowery pattern?

They were sitting so still. Nick had never known anyone his own age who could sit completely motionless like that.

Both of them held laptops against their knees, and maybe their eyes flicked back and forth, reading the screens. But they were both turned sideways, so Nick couldn't tell for sure.

"It's definitely them, right?" Nick whispered to Eryn.

She nodded without glancing his way.

Nick wasn't sure why he'd had to ask. Both Ava and Jackson looked exactly like the pictures back at Mom and Michael's house. Nick didn't have any way to measure it, of course, but he would have said their hair was exactly the same length; the scar in Jackson's eyebrow was just as distinct.

Why did that seem odd?

Nick heard footsteps inside the house and ducked his head down. Then curiosity got the better of him, and he peeked over the window ledge again.

A woman was standing in a doorway behind Ava and Jackson. She had the same reddish hair as Ava, but hers was even longer, falling in waves halfway to her waist. She was wearing a thick green sweater over a pair of jeans that looked strangely tattered and worn for someone who owned such frilly, prissy couches.

Evidently she'd just called out to Ava and Jackson, because they finally moved—finally proved themselves capable of movement—by turning to face her.

"Keep watching," Nick whispered to Eryn. "I'll listen."

He turned his head to press an ear rather than his eyebrows against the glass.

"—work on your research for those essays," the woman was saying, her voice distant and swimmy through the glass. "I want to see true, high-quality sixth-grade work."

So they're in sixth grade like Eryn and me? Nick thought. *They really are the same age as us?*

The woman was still talking.

"I'm going to chop vegetables for the soup. Doesn't this cold weather make you want soup?"

Nick didn't hear Ava or Jackson answer, but they'd probably just grunted or shrugged. That's what Nick did when Mom asked stupid questions like that.

He heard footsteps again, like the woman was walking away.

He went back to looking in the window. Ava and Jackson didn't move. Ava and Jackson didn't move. Ava and Jackson didn't move.

"Oh, this is thrilling," Nick complained to Eryn.

"Wait," Eryn whispered back. "I'm thinking."

"Think about the fact that we don't have forever," Nick said. "Think about the fact that if we aren't back home before Mom and Michael get there, they'll kill us. We'll be grounded until we're thirty."

"We won't ever turn thirty if they kill us," Eryn said.

"Exactly. So we'd be grounded forever."

But Eryn probably didn't hear his witty comeback, because just then a blast of music came from the back of the house—probably from the kitchen where the woman had gone to chop vegetables. It was one of those old songs Mom and Dad listened to, something from when they were in college. Nirvana? Smashing Pumpkins? Beastie Boys? It all sounded the same to Nick.

Whatever it was, it was *loud.* It was loud enough that the woman wouldn't be able to hear anything from the living/family room, not even if Ava and Jackson screamed.

Probably not, anyway.

Nick started shimmying away from the window and out from under the evergreen.

"Where are you going?" Eryn whispered.

"To meet Ava and Jackson," Nick said. He stood up. "What else did we come all this way for? I'm going to knock on the door."

SEVENTEEN

"Wait for me!" Eryn called after Nick. She wiggled out from under the tree too.

We're both totally covered in snow, and that's a problem, she thought. *This is all going to be a shock for Ava and Jackson, so we'll have to be the ones thinking clearly. We can't let them invite us into the house, not even just into the foyer, because then all the snow will melt on the floor and Ava and Jackson's mom will be suspicious unless they clean it up perfectly. . . .*

Nick reached the front porch, and Eryn stepped up behind him only a split second later. She reached toward the doorbell, then froze.

"No, no—that might be loud enough for the mom to hear," Nick warned her. "It might make its sound all over the house."

"That's what I just figured out," Eryn whispered back.

She didn't know why she was whispering. They *wanted* to attract Ava and Jackson's attention.

Nick pulled off his glove and tapped his fist gently against the wooden door.

Nobody came. Eryn could still hear music blasting from the back of the house.

"We have to knock louder," Eryn said, trying with her own fist.

Nothing.

"What if they went back to get their mom?" Nick whispered. "What if she's the type of adult who won't even let her kids answer the door, because she's afraid they'll be kidnapped or something?"

Eryn slid down off the porch, which was easy to do with all the snow piled around it. She landed crooked, righted herself, and sprang up immediately to peer in the nearest window.

Fortunately, this one still provided a view of Ava and Jackson. They were looking up from their computers, toward the door, so obviously they'd heard the knocking. But then they glanced back and forth between the door and the doorway where the loud music came from, as if they were trying to decide what to do.

Eryn tapped on the glass and put her face close to

the window and called softly, "Hey! Open the door! We're kids, not kidnappers!"

Ava and Jackson both looked toward her. Eryn grinned, trying to look friendly and kind and harmless. She pointed toward the door and mimed opening a doorknob.

Ava's and Jackson's faces both looked blank and puzzled. Evidently they didn't recognize Eryn, but they wouldn't have much to go on: She was so bundled up that really only her nose and eyes poked out from above her scarf and below her knit cap.

Ava and Jackson stood up from the couch. They looked at each other. And then they started walking toward the door.

Eryn scrambled back up to the porch so Nick wouldn't have sole responsibility for the first part of the conversation. She yanked the scarf from around her neck and the knit hat from her head. Then she knocked her hood back, too, letting her curly hair spill out.

"What are you doing?" Nick asked.

"Making it so we're recognizable," Eryn said. "What do you bet Ava and Jackson have seen our school pictures too?"

She shoved his hood and hat back as well. His hair

stuck up all over the place, so she hastily smoothed it down and hoped hers didn't look just as bad.

Just then the door opened. Jackson stood there in the foyer, with Ava right behind him.

"Most people use the doorbell," he said.

"We didn't want to—" Eryn began, then decided her first words to them shouldn't be about sneaking around behind their mother's back. "We're Eryn and Nick!"

"Who?" Ava asked.

"You know, your stepsiblings," Nick chimed in. "Your dad just married our mom. Didn't anybody tell you about us?"

Eryn didn't know why he'd had to ask that question. The answer was clear in both kids' blank expressions: No. Nobody had told Ava and Jackson about Eryn and Nick.

EIGHTEEN

Oh brother, Nick told himself. *And we thought* Mom *handled the whole stepsibling thing in a weird way.*

"Okay, look," Nick said, holding his hands out like he was trying to keep everyone calm. "You know your dad got married, right?"

"Well, yeah," Jackson said, nodding. "Duh."

"On November first," Ava said. "He married Denise Louellen Custer Stone."

"See, you do know that!" Eryn said, her voice too bright and fake. "We're Denise Stone's kids. Now does it all make sense?"

Nick cut his eyes toward Eryn to warn her: *Don't treat them like idiots. You want them to hate us? It's not their fault if Michael and their mom kept them even more in the dark than our parents did with us.*

"We thought it was weird that Mom and Michael wouldn't tell us anything about you, and didn't want us to meet," Nick rushed to add. He smiled his friendliest smile.

At least, he hoped it looked friendly. "We didn't know why, and we figured you were curious about us, too, and—"

"Okay," Jackson interrupted. "It's nice to meet you. Thank you very much for coming. But we've got homework." He spoke in a rush, mashing his words together. Maybe he even said all of them in one breath.

Then he put his hand on the door and started to swing it shut.

Thinking fast, Nick stuck his foot out and jammed it between the door and the doorframe.

"Wait!" Eryn cried, pushing her hand against the door too. "We want to talk to you! We want to get to know you! We—"

"You can't," Ava said.

She looked down at Nick's foot like it was just a thing: an annoyance, an obstacle, a piece of trash that wasn't even worth recycling. She kicked her own foot against his. She had a surprisingly strong kick for a sixth-grade girl. She was just wearing a pair of Keds, and it still hurt. Nick jumped back, and had to resist the urge to pull off his boot and clutch his foot in his hand and hop up and down crying *ow, ow, ow!*

Then Ava and Jackson together overpowered Eryn's hold on the door too. They shut the door right in Eryn's face.

NINETEEN

"That did not go well," Nick said.

Eryn gave him her fiercest glare. It felt like her eyebrows were climbing on top of each other.

"That's not funny!" she said. "It was awful! What's wrong with them? They didn't even blink when we told them who we are. Don't they care? Do they hate us? Oh, no—what if they were lying, and just planning the whole time to tattle on us to their mom? And then she'll tell Michael and he'll tell Mom and—"

"They'd have to care, to tell anyone," Nick pointed out.

Eryn barely heard him.

"Oooh," she moaned. "What if they're telling their mom right now?"

She practically threw herself off the side of the porch, down into the snow beneath the window she'd tapped just a few moments ago. She smashed her face up against the glass once again.

Inside Ava and Jackson were walking back toward the couch where they'd left their laptops.

Sit down, Eryn thought at them. *Sit down and pick up your laptops and whatever you do, do* not *call into the kitchen for your mom. . . .*

Both Jackson and Ava stopped in front of the couch. They had their backs to Eryn, so she couldn't see their expressions. Maybe they were thinking, *Okay, that was a funny trick to play on Eryn and Nick. Now let's get back to the door before they leave, so we really can find out why their mom and our dad didn't want us to meet.*

Maybe they were thinking, *Hey, it was kind of nice to stand up and walk around and stretch our legs for a minute. We really don't want to sit back down and go back to doing homework quite yet.*

Or maybe they were thinking, *That was a weird conversation. We don't believe anything those kids told us. Mom needs to protect us from weirdos like that. Mom! Mom!*

Eryn was usually so good at figuring out what people were thinking. But she was totally mystified right now.

Jackson began nodding his head up and down, up and down. Had Ava said something that Eryn missed, and he was agreeing? Really, really, really agreeing, because he kept nodding and nodding and nodding?

Eryn felt Nick slide in beside her and smash his own face up against the glass.

"Did I miss anything?" he muttered.

"Them walking," Eryn muttered back. "Jackson nodding."

He was still nodding. It had crossed the boundary from being odd to being very, very odd about ten nods ago.

"Is he having a seizure?" Nick suggested. "Is it epilepsy?"

"With epilepsy I think he'd be, like, down on the ground," Eryn told him. "Totally thrashing around. Not just having one or two neck muscles acting strange and everything else being fine."

"Maybe it's just something *like* that," Nick said.

"Mom never would have said Jackson was 'different' if he had epilepsy," Eryn retorted. "She would have bent over backwards to make sure we were being sensitive and caring toward him."

Jackson was *still* nodding. Beside him, Ava cocked her head. Was she just now noticing?

"Mom!" Ava screamed. "Mom! Shut off that music and come help! Jackson's acting broken again!"

Broken? Eryn thought. She decided this was maybe a code word in Ava and Jackson's family. Evidently he had some disease or problem that Eryn couldn't recognize that made him nod too much.

The music stopped, and Ava and Jackson's mom appeared in the doorway from the back of the house. Eryn knew that she should probably duck her head down out of sight, but she really wanted to see what happened next. And she wanted to make sure that neither Jackson nor Ava mentioned Nick and Eryn.

Jackson was still nodding. His mom ran toward him.

"Reboot yourself, Jackie, honey," she cried. "Come on. You can do it."

"C-c-can't," Jackson said.

Jackson's mother reached his side and hit him on the back.

"C-c-c-c-c-c-c . . . ," Jackson said.

"Shut the blinds!" Jackson's mother screamed at Ava. "Then come back and help!"

Eryn ducked down below the level of the windowsill so quickly that she smashed her face into the snowdrift. Nick didn't react as fast. Eryn had to reach up and pull his head down too.

She crouched with her face in the snow and her

heart pounding until she heard something falling above her head and on the other side of the glass—blinds cascading down, she guessed.

Ava already knew Nick and I were out here, Eryn reassured herself. *It doesn't matter if she sees us.*

Eryn dared to lift her head again. She thought it was a hopeless move, since the falling blinds had undoubtedly blocked her view of anything happening inside. But miraculously, there was almost a full inch of uncovered glass at the bottom of the window. Maybe the blinds had caught on something. Maybe Ava had been moving too hastily to let them all the way down.

Either way, Eryn could still see what was going on inside Ava and Jackson's house.

Jackson's mom peeled off the boy's hoodie. Ava shoved her brother's T-shirt up toward his neck, so Eryn could see the boy's long, muscular back.

Is he choking? Eryn wondered. *And they're doing the Heimlich maneuver?*

Eryn was pretty sure it was only choking babies who needed to be pounded on the back—not anyone older than that. And anyhow, why would Ava and her mom need to raise Jackson's shirt to hit his back?

Jackson's mom seemed to be just tapping his back

very deliberately, in spots she measured off by spreading her fingers and rotating her hands.

And then it looked like Jackson's entire back sprang open, revealing a mass of wires and circuitry inside.

TWENTY

He's a robot? Nick thought. *Jackson's a robot?*

He glanced toward Eryn, to see if she'd figured out the same thing. Her face was suddenly, explosively red, and her eyes had shrunk into tiny slits. Her jaw dropped.

She's going to scream, Nick thought.

He clamped his hand over her mouth.

But maybe his face looked the exact same way, because at the same time she shoved her hand over his mouth.

For a moment they just stared at each other, bug-eyed. Then Nick lifted his other hand and pulled Eryn's away from his mouth. She did the same to his.

"Keep watching," she whispered.

"Right," Nick whispered back.

Jackson's mom was pulling all sorts of wires out of his back, like she was looking for the source of his malfunction. Er—was it still right to think of her as his mom if he was just a robot?

Or, what's the word for a robot that's shaped like a human? Nick tried to remember. *An android? That's not even really possible, is it? Not* this *good of an imitation. Aren't androids just imaginary? Pretend?*

Nick had never been a robotics kind of kid, so he didn't really know what was possible. He knew kids at school who were on the robotics team—but that was just about building little vehicles out of Legos and using a remote control to make them move. That wasn't someone looking and acting and seeming like a normal sixth-grade boy who was actually totally mechanical.

Or is *he totally mechanical?* Nick wondered. *Isn't there something where a person could be part human, part robot? A cyborg?*

Nick couldn't quite remember if that was the right term or not. His own brain seemed just as stuck as Jackson's. It was a little amazing that Nick wasn't stammering *c-c-c-can't b-b-b-be.*

"Help me turn him," the mom was saying to Ava inside.

She's still a mom as long as Ava's not an android or a cyborg or whatever, too, Nick told himself.

The mom and Ava shifted Jackson's body a quarter-turn, so now he had his back toward the foyer, not toward the window where Nick and Eryn were still spying. Then the mom pressed something on Jackson's side that made his whole body open up. The back half of his body stayed in place; the front half sprang to the side, facing the couch and revealing all of Jackson's innards.

Now Nick could see into Jackson's body head to toe, and it was like taking the back panel off a computer, or like looking inside a TV. Jackson was full of wires and circuitry and computer chips everywhere. There was no room left for a heart or a brain or lungs.

Okaaay, Nick told himself. *Definitely an android, not a cyborg.*

He was proud that he could be so analytical and rational, but he found that he'd pressed his gloved hand into his mouth—gagging himself this time, so Eryn didn't have to do it for him. Eryn must have had the same thought; she pressed both hands over her mouth and face, only leaving the barest gap for her eyes.

Inside, Nick noticed, Ava reacted dramatically as well, turning her head away from Jackson and shielding her eyes with her hands.

"Mom," Ava said. "Mo-om, please . . ."

The mother paused in the midst of twisting wires inside Jackson's body.

"Ava, this is nothing to become anxious about," the mother said. "It's a fact of life. You *have* to become comfortable with this."

"M-m-m-mom," Ava said, shaking her head side to side. The action was just as odd and troubled and troubling as Jackson's nodding.

"Oh, for crying out loud," the mother said. Leaving Jackson's body open and exposed, head to toe, she reached over toward Ava, lifted the back of the girl's shirt, did a series of taps—and then revealed wires and circuitry in Ava's back as well.

"Ava's a robot too," Eryn muttered. Her eyes, the only thing that showed above her gloves, were wide and shocked. "They're both robots. Mom and Michael lied. We *don't* have stepsiblings. Michael doesn't have kids. He only has robots!"

"Yeah . . . ," Nick whispered back.

He couldn't take his eyes off Ava and Jackson and their so-called mother. It was like passing a car wreck on the highway: He didn't want to look, but he couldn't look away.

"Time for some diagnostics," the mother said grimly, turning back and forth between Ava and Jackson.

No—she was nobody's mother. Not if Ava and Jackson

were both robots. She was only Michael's ex-wife.

Then the woman reached up under her shirt and touched something on her own stomach. Wires slid out, which she connected to both Ava and Jackson.

She's not Michael's ex-wife, either, Nick thought numbly. *She's another robot.*

TWENTY-ONE

Eryn gasped. It was a loud gasp, containing every bit of shock and surprise she'd been holding back since she'd first seen the wires and circuitry in Jackson's back. But she still had her hands pressed over her mouth; the winter wind still howled behind her—she thought gasping was safe.

What she really wanted to do was scream. Scream and scream and never stop.

I want my mommy, she thought, which was ridiculous. Mom would be furious if she knew where Eryn and Nick were, if she knew they'd disobeyed her and gone to meet Ava and Jackson.

Or would she, if we told her everything? Eryn wondered. *What if* Mom *doesn't even know that Ava and Jackson and their mom are robots? What if they've always acted normal around her? What if Michael's fooled her?*

Eryn had to put that thought aside, because just then

the robot mother turned her head toward the window. Had she heard Eryn's gasp? Had she suddenly realized that Ava hadn't pulled the blinds all the way down?

Either way, Eryn and Nick had to get out of sight.

Eryn smashed down into the snow, pulling Nick with her. But that wasn't enough, because what if the robot mother came over to the window to look out?

"Run!" Eryn said through gritted teeth, right into Nick's ear.

She grabbed the back of his coat and pulled him along. She wanted to make sure they stayed crouched low as long as they were near windows. They reached the tree at the side of the house, stood up, and veered diagonally across the yard.

The tree would block any view the robots have of us, wouldn't it? Eryn thought.

Now that she didn't have to crouch, she ran full speed, or as close to full speed as she could in snow boots, through knee-deep snow. She ran crazily, clutching Nick's sleeve. She wasn't sure who was pulling whom—they seemed to take turns with who was in the lead.

The wide street that had seemed so ordinary and pleasant before felt menacing and dangerous now. Why did every step seem to take forever? Why did the wind seem to howl straight into Eryn's face no matter which way she turned her head?

What if the robots—or at least the robot mom—came after Eryn and Nick? What would happen then?

Would she just tell Mom and Michael what we did? Eryn wondered, stumbling forward. *Or would she maybe . . . turn us into robots too?*

That was crazy. Probably Eryn should be more afraid of being killed. But she still found herself whimpering.

They reached the edge of Lipman Park, and Nick stumbled against one of the trees that lined the perimeter.

"Got . . . to . . . stop," he panted. "Take . . . break. Hide . . . here."

He let his forward momentum carry him around the tree trunk, to the side facing away from the street. He slid to the ground at the tree's base.

Eryn sank down beside him, even though it meant practically burying herself in snow. She leaned her head back against the tree trunk.

"We have to tell Mom," she said. It was like now that she'd stopped running, all sorts of thoughts caught up with her. "No way she would have told us we had step-siblings if she knew Ava and Jackson are just . . . *things.*"

"I bet Michael lied to her," Nick said. He snorted.

"The man's a *computer* expert. Robots are just overgrown computers. He probably goes to bed every night laughing at what a big trick he played on Mom and us."

"Not anymore," Eryn said, pulling out her phone.

We'll show Michael, she thought. *Nobody messes with* our *family.*

"I knew all along he was despicable," Nick agreed. "I just didn't know why."

"Mom will thank us for saving her," Eryn muttered, her finger hovering over two choices: Mom's cell or work number.

Cell, she thought, stabbing her finger at the screen. *I don't want to talk to her secretary. Just her.*

The phone rang. Mom picked up.

"I'm on my way," she said, without even a hello. "It's just taking forever."

"Mom, you won't believe this," Eryn said. She felt Nick beside her pressing his head against hers so he could hear too. "Michael's been lying to you all along. We met Ava and Jackson. *We* know the truth. We know they're—"

"Hang up!" Mom screamed. Eryn had never heard her sound so frightened. "Don't say anything else! Hang up and go home *right now*!"

The line went dead.

TWENTY-TWO

"That was weird," Nick said.

He really wanted to say, *That was scary*, but there were certain things you couldn't admit after about the age of seven. Fear, for example.

And yet he could feel terror coursing through him. He started shivering, and it had nothing to do with the snow packed against his back and shoulders and rump and blowing into his face.

Mom was terrified, he thought. *I've never heard her sound like that.*

That scared him even more.

Eryn bit her lip and squinted down at her phone.

"I'm calling her back," she said. "She's got to explain."

Nick shoved Eryn's phone lower, back toward her pocket.

"I think we should go home," he said. "I think something's really wrong."

"Yeah, Michael's kids and ex-wife are robots!" Eryn said. "That's really wrong!"

"Something worse," Nick said.

He stood up and put a hand out to help Eryn up too. His legs had gone stiff just from the few minutes of sitting. They were sore, too, from running through all the deep snow behind them.

Somehow the snow ahead of them looked even deeper.

"Mom needs to explain, if she knew about this all along," Eryn said angrily.

But Nick noticed that she tucked her phone back into her pocket and began taking long strides toward the center of the park. Toward home.

The park seemed to have multiplied in size since the last time they walked through it. The snowdrifts seemed exponentially deeper. And once they reached the opposite side of the park, they still had to struggle through barely passable sidewalks along one neighborhood street after another.

They were finally, wearily turning onto their own street when Nick remembered that they'd planned to go back and quickly reshovel Mr. Cohen's driveway and sidewalk.

Then he remembered that they'd left their shovels back at Ava and Jackson's house. At the robots' house.

"Oh no—our shovels!" he said.

Eryn looked down at her hands like she was surprised not to still be clutching her shovel handle.

"Who cares?" she said, shrugging. "We already told Mom we were at Ava and Jackson's house. We don't need a cover story anymore. It's not like the shovels being under that tree are going to ruin anything." Her face took on the set, stubborn expression that always meant she'd made up her mind. "*I'm* not going back for them."

There was no way Nick wanted to go back either. But he was a little shocked. Mom and Dad had always drilled into them that they needed to take good care of their possessions. He could hear Mom's voice in his mind: *It's a part of being a good steward of the Earth's resources—and of your own resources. . . .*

He and Eryn were just breaking rules right and left today. Where would it end?

They came into view of their own house. The driveway was mostly covered again; the snow and the wind had erased practically every sign that Nick and Eryn had ever shoveled. There were also no tire tracks in the snow, no interruption in the drifts blown against the garage door.

So Nick knew neither Mom nor Michael were home yet.

Oh no—how will we ever face Michael again? Nick wondered. *How could* he *ever face* us *again?*

Maybe they wouldn't have to. Maybe Mom would just quietly divorce Michael for lying, and they'd never have to see him again.

Eryn started taking long steps across the yard, even as she fumbled in her pocket for the house key. His legs ached and his muscles protested, but Nick forced himself to catch up to his sister.

Her hands shook as she tried to put the key in the keyhole.

"Here," Nick said, putting his hand over hers, helping out.

But maybe his hands were shaking too. Or maybe some sort of ice crystals had formed inside the lock, blocking the key. Because he couldn't get the key to work right either.

Suddenly the door swung open and there was Mom, dressed half in her work clothes (silky red blouse, black pants) and half in gear that would be appropriate in a blizzard (fur-lined boots and a parka.)

"M-mom?" Eryn stammered. "We didn't see your car. Or any sign of it. We thought—"

"I walked," Mom said. "I left my car in a parking lot off Apple Tree Boulevard and I walked."

Nick braced himself for Mom to start yelling at them. He braced himself for Eryn to start yelling back.

Instead, Mom left the door hanging open and stepped out onto the porch with them. And then she gathered them both into a massive hug, holding them tight against her parka and not letting go.

This definitely wasn't the way she usually hugged them when they'd done something wrong and she wanted to punish them. This was a new kind of hug, one Nick had never even had to imagine before.

This, Nick thought, *is how you hug someone you thought you'd never see again.*

TWENTY-THREE

Mom's flipping out, Eryn thought.

That was strange, because Mom *never* flipped out. She was a rock, a pillar of strength, the person you'd want beside you in any emergency. One time when Nick and Eryn were little, another kid had pushed Nick off the climbing structure at the playground. And Mom had managed to pull out all the mulch from the cuts on Nick's knees and elbows *and* scrub away all the blood *and* bandage all the wounds even as she calmly lectured the other kid about the importance of playing nice and being kind to other people and treating others as we ourselves would like to be treated.

And that was while both Nick and Eryn were screaming at the top of their lungs—Nick, because he was hurt, and Eryn, because she was worried about Nick.

So why was Mom acting crazy now? Leaving the door open, stepping outside without even buttoning her coat, abandoning her car in a terrible storm, hugging Eryn and Nick like she'd been afraid they were going to die . . .

Or maybe, is still afraid we might die? Eryn thought, her head trapped under Mom's trembling arm.

Eryn shoved away from her mother.

"Explain," Eryn said.

Mom plastered a large, fake smile on her face.

"Why don't we shovel the driveway again first, so Michael can get into the garage safely?" she asked.

Eryn wanted to scream, *Who cares? Michael's a liar! I guess maybe you already know about the robots—you're not acting like you want us to tell you—but* he *sure lied to* us! *Showing us pictures of his beloved "children" . . . The way you're behaving, isn't that proof that you've been lying too? And now you want us to act like nothing ever happened? Like we're such good, happy stepkids, eager to help our stepdad?*

Eryn would have screamed all that, except that Mom lifted her hand toward her face and touched her forefinger gently to her lips. And then, just as quickly, she put her hand down and gazed cautiously out toward the street.

Mom doesn't want anyone to see her telling us to be quiet? Eryn thought. *What's that all about?*

Eryn looked toward Nick, hoping he'd been able to figure out more than she had. He'd also pushed away from Mom's suffocating hug. He was standing with his arms crossed.

"We can't shovel the driveway," Nick said. "We lost the shovels. We left them back at Ava and Jackson's."

Mom winced.

"Right," she said, "Michael's ex-wife told me she'd found them. I talked to her right after I talked to you."

"You did?" Nick said.

That wasn't Michael's ex-wife! Eryn wanted to scream. *That was a robot!*

Mom gave a little shake of her head to both of them.

"Nick, would you go ask a neighbor if we could borrow their shovels?" she suggested in a bright, artificial voice.

"Which neighbor?" Nick asked, staring at Mom suspiciously.

"I don't care!" Mom said. "Just go!"

That wasn't like Mom either. Normally she would calculate a whole complicated rubric about which neighbor they'd borrowed from or loaned something to most recently, which neighbor acted friendliest, which neighbor would be most forgiving if something broke. . . . Eryn figured wars had been fought with less advance planning than Mom put into borrowing a wrench.

Nick stumbled off the porch and headed toward the house next door. Right now, Eryn couldn't even remember who lived there.

Mom took Eryn's arm and began tugging her toward the driveway, away from the sheltered porch and back into the wind and driving snow.

"Let's get into position so we're ready when Nick comes back," Mom said.

"Aren't you going to close the door?" Eryn said, because she could feel the heat seeping out of the house.

"Oh, right," Mom said, pulling the door shut. "This cold makes me light-headed."

So why are we still out in it? Eryn wanted to scream. But she held back because Mom obviously wanted to stay outside. Mom was the one with answers; if Eryn wanted to hear them, Eryn had to keep Mom happy.

They reached the middle of the driveway, out in the open, at the mercy of the wind and snow. And ice pellets. Eryn was pretty sure there were ice pellets mixed in with the snow hitting her face.

Mom huddled close to Eryn and cupped her hand over Eryn's ear.

"What if we agree never to speak of what you found out about Ava and Jackson?" Mom whispered. "In exchange, you could get to see them every now and then. I'm sure they'll start . . . behaving better soon. After a while, you'll forget they're . . . different."

Eryn jerked away from Mom's grasp. She wasn't cold anymore. Fury made her feel like her body temperature had quadrupled.

I have to show Mom that's not going to work, Eryn thought. *I have to show Mom she* has *to tell us. . . .*

Eryn leaned her head back and screamed up at the sky, "Listen up, everyone! My—"

Mom's hand clamped over Eryn's mouth with an iron grip before Eryn could finish her sentence: *My stepbrother and stepsister are robots!*

"My daughter and I are going to build an igloo!" Mom took over shouting at the snowy world around them, as if dozens of people were listening and hanging on to every word. She leaned closer to Eryn and whispered, "I'll tell you everything in the igloo. It'll be safe there."

Eryn narrowed her eyes at her mother.

"Promise?" Eryn asked.

"I promise," Mom whispered back.

This was *Mom.* Mom who lectured them about keeping their word, Mom who became almost physically ill in the presence of liars, Mom who was trustworthy and honorable and kind.

Eryn believed her.

TWENTY-FOUR

When Nick came back holding three shovels he'd borrowed from the Winowskis, Mom and Eryn were crouched down by the huge snow pile beside the mailbox. They seemed to be trying to hollow out the inside of the pile by hand.

"Finally!" Mom said, grabbing one of the shovels and driving its blade into the very heart of the snowdrift. "A faster method!"

"We're building an igloo before we shovel the driveway," Eryn told Nick. She leaned closer and whispered, "Mom says she'll tell us everything inside the igloo. Where it's 'safe.'"

Eryn rolled her eyes, which Nick could tell meant, *Yeah, Mom is acting totally nuts. But I'm playing along because how else are we going to find out anything? You play along too.*

"O-kay," Nick said. He thought about pointing out

that even if they succeeded in hollowing out the snow-drift, that would give them a snow cave or fort, not an igloo. An igloo involved making blocks of snow and piling them up into a dome. He'd learned that back in the days when he'd wanted to be a great explorer.

But building an actual igloo would take longer than just hollowing out a snowdrift, so he kept his mouth shut. He handed Eryn a shovel and aimed the blade of the third shovel at a spot a foot or so away from Mom.

The consistency of the snow had changed since earlier in the day. Now it was wet and heavy and hard to lift. But Nick and Eryn and Mom shoveled doggedly.

Is this just another example of Mom trying to psych us out? Nick wondered. *Is she just trying to wear us out so we forget we have lots of questions?*

Nick knew neither he nor Eryn would forget.

Finally they'd hollowed out enough space in the snowdrift so all three of them could fit inside. At least, they could all three fit if they drew their knees up to their chins and huddled together.

Mom sat in the middle.

"Now," Eryn said.

Mom looked side to side, from Eryn to Nick and back again.

"I'm endangering you," she said. "In 2014, ten kids across North America died in hollowed-out snowdrifts just like this one. In 2015, the number was—"

"Mom," Nick said. "We'll be fine."

"You *promised*," Eryn said.

It felt like they were ganging up on Mom. In an unfair way.

That didn't make Nick want to stop.

Mom sighed.

"Ava and Jackson are . . . sort of an experiment," Mom said. "That's all."

"That's *all*?" Eryn exploded, recoiling so much that her head bashed into the packed snow behind her. "You make us dig an entire igloo just to tell us that? You hang up the phone on us and act like you're handling state secrets just because of an *experiment*?"

"Um . . . they're kind of an illegal experiment," Mom whispered.

"You'd marry someone who's carrying out an illegal experiment?" Nick asked.

"Yeah, you always act like we deserve the death penalty if we so much as drop a candy wrapper on the ground and don't pick it up," Eryn agreed. "You tell us we have to follow *every* rule and law. Michael must have spent years building Ava and Jackson. If they're illegal, he must have broken the law *every single day* he went to work."

"Don't forget about Ava and Jackson's mom," Nick chimed in. "Michael must have spent a lot of time building the robot mom, too. He had plenty of time to realize he was doing something wrong. And he did it anyway."

The color drained from Mom's face, leaving her almost as pale as the snow behind her.

"You . . . you could tell that Brenda was a robot too?" she asked.

"Brenda's the mom's name?" Eryn asked.

Nick didn't need that detail worked out.

"Well, yeah, we could tell she was a robot," he said, putting a sarcastic spin on his words. "People with wires hanging out of their stomach tend to make me think that."

"Why did she have wires hanging out of her stomach?" Mom asked. Her voice came out so faintly she seemed to be struggling to make a sound at all.

"Diagnostics," Eryn said. "She was doing diagnostics on Ava and Jackson."

"Oh," Mom said. "*That's* what Brenda was trying to tell me."

She buried her face in her hands, a movement that looked like total despair.

Nick had never seen his mom in despair. She was all about looking on the bright side; seeing the glass as half-full, not half-empty; overcoming every obstacle along the way. Normally she made it sound like Nick and Eryn should be able to succeed on grit and brains and effort alone.

"If the two of you saw . . . ," Mom murmured. "Who else might have been watching?"

"We were peeking through a little crack between the bottom of the blinds and the top of the window frame," Nick said, because he was almost starting to feel sorry for Mom. "Nobody else was with us."

"Hold on," Eryn said, her hands splayed out, slamming against the wall of snow before her. She didn't sound like she was feeling sympathy for anyone. "Mom, do you even *care* about how betrayed Nick and I feel because of you and Michael lying to us? Or are you just worried about your precious Michael getting caught?"

"You don't understand," Mom said, lifting her head only a little to peek toward Eryn. "It's not that simple."

"We *want* to understand, but you won't tell us anything," Eryn complained. "What do we have to do? Threaten to go to the police?"

Would Eryn actually do that? Nick wondered.

"No!" Mom cried, her voice ringing with real fear. "I'll tell you. It's just—it's a long story . . . . You see, for centuries, humans made a series of very bad choices—"

"Don't go all the way back to the beginning of time and try to bore us to death!" Nick interrupted.

Eryn whipped out her cell phone.

"La, la, la," she said, with fake breeziness. "Nine-one-one is such an easy number to dial. . . ."

"Stop!" Mom said the panic escalating in her voice. "Look, I'll show you how serious this is. I . . ."

Oddly, she stopped talking to unzip and unbuckle her parka. It was warmer inside the snow cave than outside, but it wasn't like anyone would be sweating. Only, Mom didn't stop with the parka. She also started fumbling with the buttons on her red blouse. And then she reached inside her blouse and pulled out . . .

Wires. Now the same kind of wires dangled from Mom's stomach that had dangled from the robot mom's.

"I'm a robot too," Mom said in a pained voice. "Every adult you know is. And everyone else over the age of twelve."

TWENTY-FIVE

Eryn ran.

She didn't plan it; it just happened. One minute she was sitting there in the claustrophobic snow cave staring at the inexplicable tangle of wires spilling out of her mother's body. The next minute she was crashing her way out of the snow cave and speeding across the snowy yard. She was on the porch before she knew it, slamming against the front door, twisting the doorknob. . . .

Miraculously, both she and Mom had forgotten to lock the door.

Mom's not really Mom, Eryn reminded herself. *Mom's a robot.*

Maybe Mom had always been Mom before, but something had just happened today where she'd been replaced by a robot? A robot impostor?

Eryn ran away from those thoughts too.

Without even pulling off her snow boots—a huge

violation of one of Mom's rules—Eryn dashed through the living room and sprinted up the stairs. She turned the corner into her own room and flung herself across her bed.

"Not true," Eryn moaned. "Not, not, not, not . . ."

She might as well have been Jackson, stuck on the word *can't*.

She'd been horrified by the sight of the wires and circuitry hidden in his back—and the sight of all his inner electronics exposed, head to toe. She'd been horrified by the wires poking out of Ava's back, out of Ava and Jackson's mother's stomach. But this was so much worse. Those three people—er, robots—were nothing to Eryn. This was her own *mother.* The image of Mom with wires sticking out of her was seared on Eryn's eyeballs; it might as well be branded on her brain. She would never stop seeing it.

Dimly, Eryn heard a clatter downstairs and then on the staircase. And then Nick and Mom were rushing into her room.

"Eryn?" Nick called. "Eryn?"

Eryn couldn't tell if he'd come to console her or if he expected her to console him.

"Oh, honey," Mom wailed. "It's okay."

Eryn curled up into a very small ball on the bed, as far away from Mom as she could get. Nick circled the bed and huddled beside her.

Mom stopped running toward them. She had at least put her stomach back together before coming upstairs. She looked perfectly normal now, except that she was still wearing her coat indoors and, like Eryn's, her boots were dripping all over the floor.

Mom held her out hands flat in front of her, a calming *I come in peace* type gesture.

Wait. Was there something written on the palm of Mom's right hand?

Eryn hunched her head down lower and squinted. It looked like Mom had written "<u>Please</u> don't say anything about Ava and Jackson. Our lives depend on it."

And Mom always accused *Eryn* of being melodramatic?

Eryn kept squinting.

"Eryn, honey, I know this was a huge shock for you," Mom said, in the same kind of soothing tone Eryn would expect lion tamers to use. "I know you're just reacting in the manner of a typical tempestuous preteen. I can only imagine what you're feeling right now. But there is a lot more at stake than your own adolescent trauma. I never intended for you to see . . . what you saw. It was just the exact right combination of temperature changes and, and other forces there in our snow cave. . . .”

What was Mom talking about, that she never intended Eryn to see what she saw? Mom had deliberately unzipped her parka. Mom had deliberately unbuttoned her blouse. Mom had . . . well, whatever it took to get all those wires to burst out of her stomach.

Eryn winced, seeing the horrifying scene in her head all over again.

Mom winked at Eryn. Not a blink—a *wink*. It wasn’t a jaunty, happy-go-lucky, *we’re sharing a fun little secret* wink, either. It was a desperate, beseeching, *please, please, please don’t ruin everything* wink.

“You *will* be told everything,” Mom said, her voice still as smooth and soothing as cream. “But there’s a procedure we have to follow now, a process. You two will have to swear to follow the proper guidelines for dealing with the top-secret information you’ll have access to.”

Were they going to be sworn in to the CIA? The FBI? The NSA?

There aren’t robots who look exactly like humans in any of those agencies, are there? Eryn wondered.

Of course there were, if Mom was telling the truth

about every adult being a robot. Still, Eryn couldn't be sure. She couldn't be sure of anything right now. If Mom wasn't really Mom—and wasn't even human—then everything else Eryn believed or thought she knew was suspect too.

"What if we don't swear to that?" Eryn asked. "Or what if we make the promise but break it?"

"You don't want to know what would happen to you then," Mom said, and there seemed to be genuine sorrow and fear in her voice.

Of course, up until about five minutes ago, Eryn had believed Mom was a genuine human being, too.

"What happens next is—" Mom began, but then she broke off because the doorbell sounded downstairs.

For a second all three of them froze. The doorbell sounded again.

Mom stepped to the side, leaving a clear path out of Eryn's room.

"I'll let the two of you answer that," she said.

TWENTY-SIX

I bet it's some RoboCop police force, Nick thought. *I bet they're here to round up Eryn and me for finding out too many robot secrets.*

That was a ridiculous idea. He wanted to laugh, but it was like his brain kept whispering to him, *This isn't a joke. This is real. Oh crap, oh crap, oh crap . . .*

He couldn't have managed a chuckle if his life depended on it.

He and Eryn descended the stairs almost as if they were robots themselves. Step. Down. Step. Down. Step.

Eryn robotically scraped open the door.

A bunch of kids Nick had seen around the neighborhood were standing on the front porch. They were all holding sleds: Flexible Flyers and discs and foam boards and the inflatable rafts that looked more like something you'd take into the ocean.

"Since you're new in the neighborhood, we thought

maybe you hadn't found the sledding hill yet," a boy standing in the front said. He was just a little taller than Nick, with dark skin and dark hair smashed down under a red knit cap. "Want to go sledding with us?"

"Um," Nick said.

He couldn't think about sledding right now. All he could think was, *Is that boy a robot too?*

Mom had said everyone over the age of twelve was a robot. It wasn't like Nick could just ask this kid—or any of the kids—to whip out an ID card showing their ages. But . . .

But I've seen this kid waiting at the junior high bus stop, Nick thought. *That means he's in the seventh grade, at least. He could be thirteen.*

Nick found his gaze straying toward the boy's mid-section, the part of the body where Nick had seen Mom and Michael's supposed ex-wife reveal a jumble of wires. This boy had on one of those Columbia coats with a waterproof layer on the outside and a fleece layer inside. Was the boy's body layered too, looking perfectly human on the outside but full of wires and circuits inside?

Nick glanced past the boy, back to the other kids. Some were shorter; some were taller. Any of them could be eleven or twelve or thirteen—it was too hard to tell.

Wait. Mom said everyone over twelve was a robot, Nick thought. *That doesn't automatically mean that everyone twelve and under* isn't *a robot. It could be that there's not a single actual human being standing on our porch. It could be that there's not a single other actual human being on the entire planet except Eryn and me.*

How do I even know for sure that Eryn's not a robot too?

Nick thought he might faint.

"Th-thanks for inviting us," Eryn said. Apparently she was still capable of thinking about sledding right now. And of remembering that someone needed to give an actual answer. "But we were already outside for hours, shoveling and, and building a snow cave and all. I think we're just going to stay inside now, drinking hot chocolate. Maybe another time?"

Eryn sounded like she herself might pass out or vomit. But she was saying all the right words.

The boy in the red knit cap shrugged.

"Sure," he said. "Another time. Or, if you guys warm up for a while and then want to come out, just let us know. Here. This is my cell number. I'm Milo."

Milo scrawled something on a piece of paper he took from his pocket and handed it to Eryn.

Eryn blushed.

"Okay," she said. "Thanks."

Hello? Nick wanted to shout at her. *Don't go falling in love or anything! He's a robot!*

Somehow Nick felt sure of that now.

"Okay," Milo repeated, his eyes on Eryn's face. Then he darted his gaze toward Nick. "Later, dude."

The cluster of kids with sleds began turning around and stepping down off the porch. Mom came up behind Eryn and Nick and gently eased the door shut after a mumbled "Bye, kids."

Then Mom gathered Eryn and Nick into another hug. This one didn't seem quite as desperate as the one she'd given them out on the front porch. But it was still intense.

"In case you didn't figure it out, that was a test," Mom said. "You both passed."

"They were all robots, weren't they?" Eryn asked. "I think there's a way to tell. Something about the eyes . . ."

Nick noticed that Mom didn't answer.

"Who set up that test?" he asked. "And what would have happened if we'd failed? Are there still more tests ahead? More ways for us to fail?"

Mom's face looked as pale as she'd looked in the

snow cave, when she'd seemed to match the color of the snow.

"Maybe it would be best for you just to listen," she said. "And not ask any more questions."

Eryn's wrong about what marks somebody as a robot or not, Nick thought. *It's not the eyes. It's saying stuff like that.*

How could any human being *not* ask questions at a time like this?

TWENTY-SEVEN

"We'll take you downtown where the officials will tell you everything you need to know," Mom said. "I think we should just wait until the morning, when Michael and your father can go with us. And when you've calmed down a little."

"We won't be any calmer then," Eryn said. "We'll just be more . . ."—she chose one of Mom's favorite words—"more agitated. Keyed up. We won't be able to sleep tonight and so we'll just be crazy hyper tomorrow. We won't be able to listen to anything anyone says."

It was odd how, now that she'd seen the wires hanging from Mom's stomach, Eryn could also see how slightly off Mom's eyes were.

No, not just her eyes, Eryn told herself. *Her entire face.*

It was not as extreme as the difference between a doll's face and a child's, but there was a deadness to Mom's gaze that Eryn had never noticed before.

No, I did notice it, Eryn realized. *I just thought that was how adults looked. I thought that would happen to my face too, once I grew up.*

She'd always just thought that adults were bigger and stronger and wiser and had calmer faces and flatter eyes.

What if every single bit of that was a sign of fakeness?

"Mom, take us downtown now," Nick said. "Give us the answers we need. Before we—"

"All right!" Mom said. "I will. Just . . . let me figure out what to do about a car."

It was only then that Eryn remembered Mom had abandoned her car in a parking lot off Apple Tree Boulevard, to get home to Nick and Eryn as quickly as she could.

Eryn caught herself feeling guilty that Mom had walked all that way in the cold. It made her feel guilty that she and Nick were acting so demanding and bratty now.

But what if robots don't even feel cold? She wondered. *What if that's all been an act?*

What if robots can't feel anything? Not cold, not heat, not love, not hate . . .

How could Eryn have parents who didn't even love her?

"Which of our neighbors would loan you their *car* in this weather?" Eryn asked, because it was easier to think about cars than love right now.

"I can't ask," Mom said, turning abruptly, as if she was the one who was agitated. "We'll have to walk back to the boulevard and go from there."

So that's what they did. Mom insisted on dropping off the Winowskis' three shovels on the way. Mr. Winowski accepted them with a grin and a hearty "No problem! It just meant we could postpone shoveling our own driveway!"

Eryn stared at his eyes. His were dark gray and just as flat and dull as Mom's. But something about them made Eryn think, *He knows. He already found out somehow that Nick and I know the big secret, and so this is all just one big charade. . . .*

Eryn wanted to blurt, *Can't you all just stop acting?* But just then little Amie Winowski came to the door behind her father. She wrapped her little toddler arms around his knees and gazed adoringly up at her father's face.

"My Da-Da," she said, as if to warn Eryn and Nick not to try claiming him for themselves.

I used to look at Dad exactly like that, Eryn thought. *And that's real to Amie. Real emotion. Even if everything else is fake, how can I start screaming in front of a little kid?*

She and Nick let Mom do all the talking.

After a few moments they were back to trudging through the snowdrifts, then across an open field. Eryn's legs already ached from the long walk earlier in the day and all the shoveling and digging they'd done. But she didn't complain.

She had the feeling walking through the deep snow was still easier than what they were going to face downtown.

They finally reached the car, and of course it was coated with snow and ice.

"Get in," Mom said. "I'll scrape the windows. But—be careful what you say inside the car."

She pointed to her gloved hand, and Eryn wondered if the skin underneath still contained the words "Please don't say anything about Ava and Jackson. Our lives depend on it." Wouldn't Mom have washed that off if she wanted to keep secrets?

Where was the danger coming from? How could Mom be afraid of what Eryn and Nick might say sitting alone in her car?

Could the car and the house be *bugged*?

Eryn slid in on the stiff, cold car seat and let Mom

close the door beside her. She and Nick exchanged nervous glances, but neither of them said a thing.

Mom finished chipping away at the ice and snow and slipped into the driver's seat.

"At least we'll be going against traffic," she said. "At least everybody who could just stayed home today, or has already gotten home, or . . ."

It wasn't like Mom not to finish a sentence.

"I think this storm was worse than people expected," Nick ventured, and Eryn was impressed that he could make an attempt at conversation at a time like this. Even if it was a really lame attempt.

"Sometimes it's hard to know what to expect," Mom said, and it didn't seem like she was just talking about the weather.

Mom inched the car forward, through the snowy parking lot and out onto the snowy boulevard. Eryn didn't know how anyone could stand to go so slow. If Eryn had been old enough to drive, she'd be smashing her foot against the accelerator right now; she'd risk skidding and careening if it meant she could get to answers sooner.

But Mom already knows all the answers, Eryn thought. *Doesn't she?*

Finally, after what seemed like an eternity, Mom

pulled into the parking garage under City Hall. It felt strange to be away from the constant beating of snowflakes against the car windows. The windshield wipers squeaked against the suddenly bare glass.

Mom parked in the first space she came to and turned off the car.

"Michael said he would meet us here, but I don't see him yet . . . ," Mom said, letting her words trail off.

Eryn realized she hadn't seen Mom call Michael.

Maybe she did that while I was putting my coat on, Eryn thought. *Or maybe it was when Mom was walking behind us in the snow.*

She'd just discovered that her mother was a robot. She wasn't willing to accept that her mother and her stepfather might communicate by telepathy, too.

"I don't want to wait for Michael," Nick said. "If he drives as slow as you, it could take him hours to get here."

Normally Mom would have answered a comment like that by firmly putting Nick in his place, telling him it was up to adults, not kids, to make decisions like that.

But now she just reached over and opened the car door.

"You'll be meeting the mayor," she said. "Please . . ."

Normally she would have finished with *be on your best behavior,* or the slightly less positive *don't say or do anything that would lead to a very serious talk about manners afterward.*

But now all she said was "Be careful."

TWENTY-EIGHT

When Mom, Eryn, and Nick stepped off the elevator in the City Hall lobby, the mayor was standing there waiting for them. She was a tall, powerful-looking woman with a severely angled haircut, and she wore the same kind of suit as Mom—the kind that seemed like a Professional Woman uniform. Nick thought maybe he'd seen the mayor on TV, at the grand opening of the library renovation or at news conferences explaining the latest city budget. The kind of television programming that Nick generally avoided or ignored.

Nick had not quite gotten what Eryn meant about adults' eyes looking different, but it made more sense to him as he gazed at the mayor. She looked plastic.

But . . . isn't that just how politicians are*?* He wondered.

The mayor stuck out her hand to shake.

"I'm Mayor Nancy Waterson," she told Eryn and

Nick, pumping their hands up and down in turn.

To Mom, she said, "I'm so sorry," in the exact tone that someone might use at a funeral, offering condolences.

Incredibly enough, Mom shrugged. Nick could practically quote Mom's lecture on that topic verbatim. ("In polite society, raising and then lowering your shoulders does *not* qualify as actual language, young man. It does not pass for a yes or a no or even an 'I don't know.' You have to use *words*. You have to state what you think and feel politely and coherently. Shrugs don't count!")

Mayor Waterson raised an eyebrow.

"We all knew it was going to happen eventually," Mom said, with such weariness that Nick wondered if the long walk through the snow had been even harder on her than it'd been on him and Eryn. "That's why we have the protocol."

"Yes, but *here*?" The mayor said. "In Maywood? I always suspected the first case, when it came, would be in New York City. That or some other place where cynicism is part of the culture."

"There are smart kids in Maywood, too," Mom said. "And it *is* a matter of intelligence, more so than cynicism. That's just one of the paradoxes we've always had to deal with, that our original programming forced us to encourage some of the very traits—curiosity and intellectual inquiry—that could eventually lead to such . . . complications and challenges."

Is Mom bragging about how smart Eryn and I are? Nick wondered. *Or . . . apologizing?*

He couldn't think about that very deeply because he got caught on one of her other words.

Programming? He thought. *Of course robots can be programmed but . . . was* Mom? *And . . . Dad? Was he "programmed," too?*

The mayor led them into a conference room at the back of the building. She pressed a button on the wall to lower all the shades.

"A historic moment," she said. "The first viewing."

What was she talking about?

"Nancy," Mom said, "you're not running for anything." She tilted her head to indicate Eryn and Nick. "They're not old enough to vote."

"And yet we're about to give them power over all of us," the mayor murmured, still sounding as though she were commemorating a historic milestone.

Power? Nick thought. *We're kids. We don't have any power.*

To cover his confusion, he focused on peeling his coat off and shoving his gloves and hat into the pockets. Mom took his coat and Eryn's and laid them across an empty chair.

Just the kind of thing she'd normally do, Nick thought. *Watching out for us. Keeping track of our stuff.*

But he noticed that Mom didn't take her own coat off, even as she and the mayor sat down. Why did that make him feel like Mom was prepared to bolt if she had to?

Not Mom, he told himself. *She wouldn't leave us behind.*

The mayor pressed another button, and a screen came sliding down at the front of the room. The lights dimmed.

"They need fingerprint authentication," the mayor said, holding out a pad to both Nick and Eryn.

Nick hesitated, wondering if he dared make a joke about needing a lawyer present before being finger-printed. He glanced sideways at Mom, whose face had settled into rock-hard grimness.

No, I don't dare, he thought.

He pressed an index finger against the pad, and Eryn did the same.

Immediately a video began on the screen, showing a man and a woman sitting at an ordinary-looking table. The people looked ordinary, too. The man had on a white lab coat. The woman was wearing blue jeans and a flannel shirt and had her dirty-blond hair pulled back into a ponytail.

"If there is someone out there to watch this video, then our plans have succeeded," the woman said.

"We thank you," the man said. "Thank you for everything you're going to do to continue to make it all work."

"And thank you to those who raised you," the woman said. She seemed to be staring over Nick's and Eryn's heads, almost as if she knew Mom would be sitting just beyond them.

"Thank you—" the woman paused, as if temporarily overcome by emotion. "Thank you for bringing the human race back from extinction."

TWENTY-NINE

"What? Extinction? That's crazy!" Nick exclaimed, jerking back in surprise and jarring against the table. He knocked it two or three inches closer to the screen. "Is this some kind of joke?"

Doesn't he see that nobody's laughing? Eryn thought numbly. *Doesn't he see that nobody's jumping out from a hidden door, yelling "Ha-ha! Fooled you! You should see your faces!"*

Eryn was so stunned she just felt paralyzed. But she managed to move her head, turning it left and right, hoping she *would* see someone jumping out and yelling *Ha-ha! Fooled you!*

She saw only Mom and the mayor, their faces sinking even further into grimness.

"So it's true," the mayor murmured. "What they told us wasn't just a programming error."

"Did you ever really believe it *could* be a mistake?" Mom said disdainfully.

On the screen, the man and the woman hesitated before they spoke again, as if they knew they had to allow a certain amount of reaction time.

"I'm Annalies Grimaldi, PhD, professor of robotics at the Massachusetts Institute of Technology," the woman said.

"And I'm Dr. Dylan Speck," the man said. "Former head of the medical school at Johns Hopkins University. Current director of the Center for Reproductive Medicine."

Both of them glanced to the side then, and flinched as if they'd seen or heard something threatening. Eryn found herself wishing that the camera had followed their gazes, or that the microphone recording their voices had been sensitive enough to pick up every sound.

Or maybe she didn't wish that. Dr. Grimaldi and Dr. Speck both looked unbearably sad.

"It has become undeniably clear to us and our colleagues—and to all our fellow human beings—that our days are numbered," Dr. Speck said. "There is no longer any hope for us."

"But how could we stand to see humanity end completely?" Dr. Grimaldi asked, the ache in her voice almost a palpable thing.

"It's too late to save ourselves," Dr. Speck said. "But

we're hoping that our two fields of professional inquiry, linked together, can provide one last chance for humanity itself."

Eryn was having a little trouble following their conversation, but she didn't think it was because she was listening to two professors. She was used to Mom using big words; she was used to hearing Michael throw around all sorts of technical computer terms.

No, it was the weight of sorrow in these people's voices that threw her off. She had never heard an adult sound so despairing.

These aren't robots, she realized.

Somehow she was certain of that, even without peering closely at the two people's eyes. For all she knew, this video was of the last two adults in the world who hadn't been robots.

"We've told you who we are—I wish we could know who we're talking to," Dr. Grimaldi said wistfully.

"We would like to believe that we are talking to perhaps an eighteen-year-old who's reached a well-adjusted adulthood full of thoughtful, reasonable questions after a safe, happy childhood," Dr. Speck said.

"But we're well aware that the slightest miscalculation on our part—especially on my part—could have led to an entirely different scenario," Dr. Grimaldi said. "We may have set up the human race to fail again, with no hope of another chance."

"Eryn and Nick are too young!" the mayor said, half standing as though she planned to shut off the rest of the video. "They're years ahead of schedule!"

"The doctor said *perhaps* an eighteen-year-old," Mom reminded her. "Eryn and Nick have questions now. They can't wait another six years."

Eryn was glad Mom understood at least that much about her and Nick.

The mayor sank back into her chair, and the video continued.

"If you are coming of age in the midst of wars or famines or a struggle against a repressive government, then—" Dr. Speck began.

"Then we are so sorry," Dr. Grimaldi finished for him. "Please don't give up. Even in these, our final days, we still have faith in the promise of humanity and human lives, and we hope that you do too."

Wars? Eryn thought. *Famines?*

Why were they talking about things that had happened only long ago in the past, or only in faraway countries?

Eryn guessed these two people would think she and Nick had had safe, happy childhoods.

"Here's what we did," Dr. Speck said. But then he stopped and looked over at Dr. Grimaldi with a bemused twist to his face. "It just occurred to me—what if we're talking to a five-year-old? What if the unanswerable questions kick in and trigger the first showing of this video much earlier than we expect? I feel like I'm explaining the birds and the bees to my kids all over again!"

"You're a doctor of reproductive medicine," Dr. Grimaldi said wryly. "You can handle it."

For adults, they were so . . . loose. So different from Mom, who always acted so rigid and so certain that everything she did was right. Even different from Dad, who was more laid-back, but thought nothing of cleaning a toilet at three a.m. if the mood struck him.

Dr. Speck shook his head and looked back at Eryn and Nick. Eryn knew he was really just looking at a camera, but somehow it felt more personal than that.

"Years before we, ah, planted the seeds of our own destruction," he said, "humanity had found new ways to deal with the problems of infertility. That's what you call it when people who want to have children discover that they can't."

"I think we could have figured that out," Nick muttered beside Eryn.

Eryn wasn't going to admit that she kind of appreciated the definition. She'd heard the word *fertile* before, but she'd thought it only had to do with growing food. Hadn't there been something called the Fertile Crescent her social studies teacher talked about at school?

"Scientists like myself figured out how to develop and freeze embryos for future use by infertile couples," Dr. Speck continued.

"What—you're not going to define embryos as, let's say, the seeds of a new human being?" Dr. Grimaldi teased. "Putting it in language a five-year-old can understand?"

"I have decided to believe that I am talking to a teenager," Dr. Speck said, with an air of insulted dignity that somehow seemed just as much of a joke. "And that you have programmed your robots to do a good job of providing appropriate background information to children at every level."

Dr. Grimaldi snorted.

"I'll add that to my list of things to double-check," she said. "There are a million items on that list—what's one more?"

If these doctors—these human beings—really thought they were only days away from destruction, how could they joke around like this? How could they laugh?

Mom doesn't have much of a sense of humor even when she isn't staring destruction in the face, Eryn thought.

On the screen, Dr. Speck rolled his eyes.

"It was always seen as a problem that certain infertility treatments generally produced many, many more frozen embryos that a typical couple would use," he continued. "Most Americans, for example, would want no more than two or three children, but when they were done having babies, they might have another eight or ten frozen embryos left in the embryo bank."

"Please don't go into that whole debate about whether a frozen embryo counts as a human being, with all the rights of a human being," Dr. Grimaldi begged. "Time is running out—remember? I don't want to spend any of my remaining life on debates that humans fought about for decades!"

"But it was that debate that kept so many frozen embryos alive," Dr. Speck said. "There were so many parents who had beloved children who had once been frozen embryos, and a lot of those parents found that they couldn't bear to let their remaining frozen embryos be thrown away like so much garbage. They kept paying the embryo banks to keep them alive. Even though, legally, they would have been well within their rights to have those embryos destroyed."

"Oh," the mayor said suddenly, jolting the table just as much as Nick had. "Really? They didn't have laws against embryo destruction? And yet they programmed us to treat every last embryo as the most precious thing ever?"

Mom frowned at her.

"Surely even a politician can figure out the psychology of that," Mom said icily. "Because those embryos became humanity's only hope."

"Why are we even talking about embryos?" Nick asked in a petulant voice that made him sound younger than twelve. Nick always sounded younger when he got tired and grumpy. Twelve years of growing up together meant that Eryn could recognize every single one of Nick's moods. And now he had shifted into his *this is boring* mode, his *can we just skip ahead to part I'm interested in?* mode.

I know what he's thinking because of the whole twin thing, too, Eryn thought.

But just the little bit of the video she'd seen so far made that thought twist in her mind. Mom and Dad were robots. She and Nick weren't. If Mom and Dad weren't really her parents, was it possible that Nick wasn't really her twin, either? Was it possible that he wasn't even her real brother? The two of them certainly looked alike, but how . . .

The truth hit her hard. She couldn't hold it in.

"Nick, they're talking about those frozen embryos because they're us," Eryn cried. "We're them. That's where we came from!"

THIRTY

Nick blinked.

"You mean Mom and Dad had to have some kind of weird infertility treatment to have us?" he asked. "I really didn't need to know that!"

Eryn whacked him on the arm, a little too hard to count as playful.

"Think!" she told him. "Mom and Dad are robots! We're human! We don't have their genes! I bet they don't even have genes to give us! So they had to get us from somewhere! And that somewhere must have been—"

"One of those frozen embryo banks," Nick finished for her.

He wanted to add *Okay, whatever. Can we never talk about this again?*

But his brain seemed to be thawing out—maybe twelve years late from being a frozen embryo.

This wasn't something he could say *whatever* to.

"So a lot of people died somehow," he said. "Maybe everyone. But those two people—" he pointed at the screen, where the video still played—"they and maybe some other scientists did something to make sure the leftover frozen embryos stayed alive. And then, when it was safe, I guess, robots they'd left behind took the embryos out of the freezer and let them grow into kids? Like, like . . ."

He couldn't quite bring himself to say *Like us*.

"Yes," Mom said, nodding gently. "The two of you started out as those frozen embryos. So did just about every kid you know. The ones who are twelve and under began that way."

Nick heard Mom speak, but he couldn't make sense of her words.

Evidently Eryn could.

"So we're just some sort of *science* experiment?" Eryn wailed. "We don't even *have* real parents? We don't have—"

"I gave birth to you," Mom said, and now there was a steeliness to her voice. "I may not be human, you may not be genetically mine, but I did give birth to you. We were designed to be able to do that. That, and other normal human activities. And your father and I—and

Michael—we've raised you. That still makes us your parents."

Eryn and Mom seemed poised for one of their mother-daughter spats, where Eryn would get more and more upset, and Mom more and more calm, until it seemed like Eryn was molten fury and Mom was so chill she didn't even have a pulse.

Mom's a robot, Nick thought. *She really doesn't have a pulse.*

Nick couldn't look at Mom right now. He swiveled his head back toward the video still playing on the screen.

"We knew it was possible to fully automate the care and maintenance of the frozen embryos—or the 'Snowflakes,' as they began to be called," Dr. Speck was saying. "'Snowflakes' because they're frozen—get it?"

"Dylan, there's no need to explain nerdy science humor," Dr. Grimaldi said, rolling her eyes. "It wasn't even funny *before* the threat of extinction."

"When we began to plan Project Return of the Snowflakes—a name I shouldn't have to explain—we had to improve our freezing techniques to ensure that the embryos would last in good health for as long as it took for the danger to pass," Dr. Speck said. "Obviously, this was one of the many aspects of the project that we couldn't test ahead of time. We just had to hope that everything would work out, centuries into the future."

"Centuries?" Eryn repeated. Apparently she'd managed to hold off on fighting with Mom, and was watching the video again now too. "They kept us frozen for centuries? Those people died centuries ago?"

The video had only been playing for ten or fifteen minutes, and yet Eryn made it sound like Dr. Speck and Dr. Grimaldi were people she'd known, people she now grieved for.

"We also didn't want humanity to be forced to start over from, say, the caveman era," Dr. Grimaldi added. "What if Humanity 2.0 simply repeated our mistakes, and crawled out of the muck to reach technological advancement only to fail again in exactly the same way?"

Personally, Nick liked the term *Humanity 2.0* better than *Snowflakes. Snowflakes* made it sound like all of them could melt away so easily the next time the weather changed.

Maybe that was the point.

"Also, our ancestors had mined out all the easily available metals and minerals that enabled them to advance," Dr. Speck said grimly. "It would be quite possible that our Snowflakes wouldn't even get out of the Stone Age."

"So some of the best minds of our generation studied exactly where we'd gone wrong," Dr. Grimaldi said. "How far back in history would we have to go to find a point where it was still possible to avoid the mistakes humanity made the first time around, leading to our inevitable destruction?"

"They settled on the early twenty-first century," Dr. Speck said.

"But—that's now!" Nick blurted out.

Eryn flashed him a disgusted look.

"Of course it is," she said. "Because this is the twenty-first century the second time around." She gazed toward Mom and the mayor. "If everyone older than twelve is a robot, then Nick and I are in the oldest group of Snow flakes, aren't we? We're among the first of the experiment, right?"

Mom nodded slowly.

"You are," she said, seeming to speak through clenched teeth.

How was Eryn figuring out everything so quickly, while Nick might as well be one of those cavemen still crawling around in the muck? His brain mostly kept sputtering out, *This can't be true, none of this can be true. . . .*

But what if it was?

"Okay, okay," Nick said, holding out his hands like he was trying to stop everything—or maybe just stop Eryn from jumping ahead of him again. "Let's cut to the important question. What do we have to do to keep from having everybody go extinct all over again?"

He saw Mom and the mayor exchange glances.

"We don't know," Mom said faintly.

"Nobody ever told us," the mayor added.

THIRTY-ONE

"Nobody ever told you?" Eryn repeated. "Didn't you ever ask?"

"Who do *we* have to ask?" Nick asked. "The governor? The president?" He narrowed his eyes at the mayor. "Do *you* know a way to call one of them to find out?"

"We always assumed the answer would be in this video," Mom said, almost as if she were the mayor's spokesperson. Or the president's.

"But you never watched the video before, just on your own? Just to find out?" Eryn asked.

The mayor and Mom both shrugged, almost as if the move had been choreographed.

"We were instructed not to do that," Mom said.

"It was in our programming that we had to wait for the first child who began asking the right questions," the mayor said.

What was our trigger question? Eryn wondered.

Was it something like "Why are there wires hanging out of Mommy's stomach?" Or "Why's the rest of our step-father's family all robots?"

That stopped her. Because, even as upset as she was, she remembered how anguished Mom had been, pleading with Nick and Eryn to keep their knowledge of Ava and Jackson secret. Mom lifted her hand slightly—helplessly—and Eryn could see just the ghost of a smudge where the words "Please don't say anything about Ava and Jackson. Our lives depend on it," had once been written.

Nick and I probably didn't ask the exact right question to get to see this video, Eryn thought. *Not on our own. Mom just set everything up by showing us the wires in her stomach and acting like we'd seen that by mistake, and so we had to watch the video. Did she do that just to stop us from asking more about Ava and Jackson?*

How could asking questions about Ava and Jackson be worse than this?

Mom's eyes met Eryn's, and Eryn winced. It seemed like Mom was still trying to say *Don't tell, don't tell, be careful . . .*

"I guess we just have to watch the rest of the video," Eryn huffed.

Dr. Grimaldi was talking about how hard everyone

had worked to replicate the world of the early twenty-first century, how they'd programmed robots to restore buildings and raise children and fake the appearance of normal human society.

"Of course, we're still very human," Dr. Speck interjected. "We couldn't resist some tinkering. When we saw the opportunity to make improvements, we did try that. For example, if everything worked as planned, you have grown up in a world without poverty, racism, sexism, or child abuse."

The only one of those terms Eryn had ever heard before was *poverty*.

"We have people who are poor," she protested.

Mom snorted.

"Not like there used to be," she said. "Everyone you've ever met has enough money to eat and to live in a decent home. You think people are poor if their kids can only afford four days a week of after-school activities, instead of five."

How much poorer could people possibly be? Eryn wondered.

On the screen, the two doctors seemed to have moved on to another topic.

"We tried to be careful, though, knowing that the next

generation would be entirely human, not to set up some impossible standard of robotic perfection," Dr. Grimaldi added. "For example, we easily could have ensured that every Snowflake grew up in a two-parent, married-couple household. But we wanted to model the possibility of divorced parents who are civil to each other too."

"Because, how could we not try to model the example of people recovering from their mistakes?" Dr. Speck said. "Us, of all people?"

Eryn could tell that he'd shifted once again, from talking about marriage and divorce to the frozen embryos and the end of human extinction. She wasn't quite so ready to move on.

"Then . . . then . . . you and Dad *could* have stayed married?" she asked Mom.

Mom tilted her head.

"It wasn't how we were programmed," she said. Then, as if flipping a switch, she went back to her usual middle-school-psychologist soothing voice: "Divorced parents can still provide loving homes for their children. Indeed, such families might increase their offsprings' resilience and adaptability—"

"But we didn't *have* to go through that," Eryn said. The excuse her parents always gave for their divorce swam in her mind—the whole head-versus-hands thing. It was all a lie. "The problem wasn't that you didn't love each other anymore. We could have had you and Dad both with us all the time. We wouldn't have ever had to leave in the middle of holidays to go to the other parent. We didn't have to always be torn in two!"

Mom just looked at her blankly.

"But we were programmed to be divorced parents. Good divorced parents. So you did have to go through that," Mom said.

That wasn't what I meant, and you know it! Eryn wanted to yell at Mom.

But maybe Mom really didn't know what Eryn meant. Maybe she wasn't capable of it.

On the screen Dr. Speck and Dr. Grimaldi were giving more details about Project Return of the Snowflakes. It was all dry, logistical information—how Dr. Grimaldi had planned and arranged for an army of robots to become the most skillful parents ever; how Dr. Speck had arranged for the stored embryos to be unfrozen and born and raised in orderly waves over the course of more than thirty years. Dr. Speck had planned for the last of the Snowflakes to be born about the same time some of the oldest Snowflakes started having children of their own, but he'd done scientific calculations so the birth rate would stay steady during that transition. And then eventually all the Snowflake embryos would be used up, and the robot parents wouldn't be necessary anymore. It would only be real, live human beings giving birth to more humans.

Eryn hoped Nick was paying better attention than she was. Maybe she was slipping into shock. She couldn't seem to listen to anything new. She couldn't seem to get past the same handful of thoughts playing again and again in her brain: *Mom and Dad are really robots? Really?* And *They didn't even have to be divorced. This is all a setup.* And *But this still doesn't explain about Ava and Jackson. Why are they illegal? If there are other robot kids—everyone older than twelve—then why are Ava and Jackson such a big secret?*

It was this last question that finally forced Eryn to pay closer attention, because she heard Dr. Grimaldi say "robot children."

"Of course, we plan to phase out those fake robot children at every childhood age and stage as the real human children reach it," she said. "And we will use the same principle for the robots in every stage of young adulthood, middle age, and elder years."

"So," Dr. Speck said, "within a century or so, we can

once again have a fully functioning, fully human society."

"Really, this is not much different from the passage of any generation," Dr. Grimaldi said, though her face seemed contorted with worry even as her voice sounded bland and soothing. "One generation passes away as the next one comes up behind it. . . . You are simply the next generation after the robots."

Mom made a tiny sound in the back of her throat, almost like a whimper. But when Eryn turned toward her, Mom just said, "No generation wants to think about passing away."

On the screen Dr. Speck and Dr. Grimaldi squared their shoulders as if they were almost done and preparing to say good-bye.

"So you see, we are placing all our hopes in you," Dr. Speck said. "We would love to give advice, but we have no idea what issues you might be facing now. So all we can say is, please, consider your future carefully."

"It is the future of our entire species, all of humanity," Dr. Grimaldi added solemnly.

"God bless all of you," Dr. Speck said. "God bless and preserve each and every one of you."

And then the screen went dark.

Eryn whirled around toward Nick.

"Wait—did I miss something?" she asked. "What did they say was going to make them extinct? What are we supposed to do to keep from becoming extinct all over again?"

"They . . . they didn't say," Nick said.

He looked so dazed Eryn wondered if he'd been in shock and not listening well either. She turned to Mom and the mayor. Both of them shook their heads.

"They didn't," Mom confirmed. "They didn't give any of that information."

"But—what happens now?" Eryn asked. "What are we supposed to do? What good does it do for them to tell us to avoid something when we don't even know what we're avoiding?"

She expected more blank looks and shrugs from Mom and the mayor. After all, they'd already said they didn't know what made humans go extinct before. But both women were eagerly leaning forward.

"This is the moment I've been waiting for, for the past twelve years," the mayor said. "The moment *after* the first viewing."

"Why?" Nick and Eryn said, practically speaking in unison.

"Because," the mayor said, "now we get to ask *you* questions."

THIRTY-TWO

"What does 'I think, therefore I am,' really mean?" the mayor asked.

"And 'To be, or not to be—that is the question,'" Mom said. "Why is that the question? Why don't humans always choose to be?"

"Why isn't the unexamined life worth living?" the mayor asked.

"And who's God?" Mom asked. "What's a soul? There's this whole category of human thought called religion—and another category called philosophy—that we've mostly just avoided dealing with because we can't understand it. Can you explain these things to us?"

"How are we supposed to know about things you grown-ups never taught us?" Nick retorted. "How are we supposed to know anything you don't know?"

"Because you're human?" the mayor said.

But it almost sounded like she wasn't sure what they were.

The door to the conference room rattled just then, making Nick jump.

Then the door opened.

It was Michael.

"What did I miss?" he asked, peering around frantically.

He's worried about Ava and Jackson, Nick thought. *More than he is about me and Eryn.*

What did that mean? That he loved them more?

Once, Nick would have thought, *Well, yeah, they're his real kids and we're not. He's only known us for a couple of years, and he's known them their whole lives.*

But now he just thought, *But they're just robots, and we're real humans!*

He thought about what he'd said to Mom and the mayor only a few moments ago: "How are we supposed to know about things you grown-ups never taught us?"

If Mom and Dad were robots and he'd spent his entire life being surrounded by robots, why did he have such a strong feeling that humans were better than robots? Why would he think that, when Mom and Dad and all his teachers and every other adult he'd ever come in contact with had told him that people with all different colors of skin were equal, and males and females were equal, and rich people and poor people were equal. . . .

Yeah, because they're all people, Nick thought. *Robots just pretend to be human.*

He didn't bother answering Michael. Eryn just pursed her lips. Mom gave a little shake of her head—so quickly that Nick thought the mayor probably didn't notice.

"We've just finished watching the video," Mom told Michael. "And Mayor Waterson and I have asked the kids some of the longstanding questions, but they said they didn't know the answers either. I think everyone's too tired to concentrate. I'm afraid you've arrived here just in time to go home."

"Oh," Michael said.

He leaned against the door, almost as if he were relieved.

Though, can a robot really feel relief? Nick wondered. *Or is he just pretending?*

Mom was right about one thing: Nick was too tired to sort out anything else about what was real and what wasn't. But he wasn't too tired to ask the big question.

"Do *you* know what happened that made humans go extinct?" he asked Michael.

Michael shook his head, throwing off little droplets

of water where the snow had melted in his hair.

It's not actually hair, Nick told himself.

"I'm sure I don't know," Michael said. "I do know nobody seems to be in danger at the present moment, so maybe it *would* be best to just go home."

Does he want to get away from the mayor, or does he want to get Eryn and me away from the mayor? Nick wondered.

Mom stood up, and the mayor did the same.

"We'll stay in touch," the mayor said. She turned to Eryn and Nick. "You two know you absolutely cannot share what you've learned today with any of your friends, right?"

"You think you're going to be able to keep this secret forever?" Eryn asked incredulously. "Secret from all the other humans, I mean. You think—"

"We think the other human children need to find out this information at their own pace," Mom said. "Just as children grow and develop at different rates, they will be ready for this potentially devastating news at different stages as they move toward adulthood. Some may never be ready."

She looked and sounded as calm as when she was explaining math homework. Except that she darted her eyes toward Michael, and then away again.

The mayor didn't seem to notice. She was peering intently at Nick and Eryn.

"And since you two are among the oldest of the Snowflakes, you must be sensitive about protecting the rights and needs of all the younger children," the mayor said. "As well as the rights and needs of the children your same chronological age who might not be as intellectually or emotionally advanced."

Nick glanced at Eryn. No matter how "advanced" they were, neither of them seemed capable of doing anything but gaping at the mayor right now. Did Nick look as much like a stupid fish as Eryn did?

"It's not like anyone would believe us anyway," Nick finally managed to mutter.

But would they?

He imagined going in to school the next day and telling everyone, *Look closely at our teachers' eyes. Notice anything weird?*

His friends would just say, *Yeah, they're grown-ups. They're teachers. Of course they're weird.*

He couldn't tell any of his friends.

"You know you can reach me any time, day or night, if you have any more questions," the mayor said, handing

Eryn a business card. "Of course, I make that guarantee to all my constituents."

Eryn did the polite thing and took the card. She shook the mayor's hand, and then everyone else did too.

"Well," Mom said. "Why don't you two kids go home with Michael, since I need to stop at the grocery to pick up a few things for dinner?"

Hadn't Mom run out to the store the night before, when she heard the weather forecast? Wasn't that what she always did when there was a storm coming?

Was she making up excuses just to get them to go with Michael? Why?

"What do you need?" Nick asked, which he was pretty sure wouldn't seem strange. He was usually interested in food.

"Milk," Mom said. "And bread."

Nick knew for a fact that there was a full gallon of milk on the top shelf of the refrigerator, and an entire loaf of bread in the pantry. But he didn't call Mom on it.

If I call her on that, what if everything else I'm wondering about comes spilling out too? Nick wondered. *What if I end up getting her arrested for hiding the secret of Ava and Jackson?*

But why were they still a secret?

THIRTY-THREE

Michael's car was parked on the street, not in the garage, so they had to trudge through more snow to get to it. Eryn barely felt the cold.

Oh, right, because how can I think about cold when I just found out that my parents are robots, and I'm some science project that came about because humanity went extinct, and my parents never even had to get divorced, except that was how they were "programmed." And, *oh yeah, my mother and stepfather did something illegal that they're worried about getting in trouble for, and our lives depend on me not telling. . . .*

Was this what it felt like to be hysterical?

Michael unlocked the car, and they all slid in onto the cold seats. Eryn took the front passenger seat; without even arguing, Nick got in back. The car had been sitting there for so brief a time that Michael only had to run the windshield wipers to clear off the snow.

"I had this car soundproofed years ago," Michael said as he cautiously pulled out into the empty, snowy street. "And the windows are specially treated so no one can see in to read our lips. So I can answer any questions you have about Ava and Jackson, and we don't have to worry about anyone overhearing or figuring out what we say."

Who would overhear us anyhow? Eryn wondered. *Who would care? The mayor? The governor? The president? Other kids? Other robot-adults? Why is Michael so paranoid he had to soundproof his car? And how could he possibly worry about people reading our lips?*

This was definitely what it felt like to be hysterical.

"How old are Ava and Jackson?" Nick asked from the backseat. "I mean, exactly. I know they're sixth graders, but . . . are they eleven? Twelve? *Thirteen?* Were they held back? Is that why . . ."

Michael shot a glance over his shoulder at Nick.

"Ava and Jackson both turned twelve on November fourth," he said in an impossibly level voice. "They're a few months younger than the two of you."

Eryn scrambled to pull her thoughts together. To think logically.

"Okay, that messes up everything I was starting to figure out," she complained. "After Mom said everyone over twelve was a robot, didn't she say everyone our age or younger is human? Wasn't that what the scientists said in the video, too? Something about robot kids being phased out as human kids grow up?"

Michael bit his lip.

"This is how the original humans set things up," he said quietly. "That's what makes Ava and Jackson illegal. There aren't supposed to be *any* robot children who are younger than the oldest human children."

"Then why don't you just say Ava and Jackson are thirteen years old?" Nick asked, leaning forward. "Why didn't you make them *be* thirteen? Then they'd be legal, right? They're just—"

Nick stopped abruptly, ending with a loud gulp. Eryn had the feeling he'd been about to say *They're just robots. Couldn't you make them any age you wanted?* Not really the right thing to say to Michael, who was also a robot.

Eryn tried to cover for her brother.

"Why did you make them, anyway, if it was illegal?" she asked. "Why take the risk? Why—"

Now she was on the verge of saying the wrong thing too. Because the next words to come out of her mouth had almost been *Why wouldn't you just do what you're supposed to do, if you're a robot? Why would you make robot children if you weren't programmed to do that?*

It was better to wait for Michael to answer the questions they'd already asked.

"I understand what you're asking," he said softly. "I don't think you understand the background."

But for a long moment, he didn't go on. He seemed to be concentrating hard on the icy street ahead of him. He was wearing his usual nerdy-professor horn-rimmed glasses; Eryn knew that under his heavy coat he had on his tweed jacket with actual patches on the elbows.

It was hard to imagine him doing anything illegal.

It was also hard to think of him as a robot. Almost as hard as it was to think of Mom or Dad that way.

Ugh. Did that mean she'd gotten used to him as a stepfather?

"How much did they actually explain in the video?" Michael finally asked. "Did they spell out what happened to all the toddler robot children the year you turned one?"

"Um . . . no?" Eryn said. "Did they, Nick? The scientists said we'd have a—what was the phrase—a fully human society?—within a century, but . . ."

She didn't want to admit she'd had so much trouble

paying attention. Maybe the scientists had explained all sorts of things she'd missed.

"I don't think they really said," Nick agreed. "Don't the robot kids just grow up ahead of us? Didn't the kids a little older than us turn two the year we turned one, then three when we turned two, then—"

"No," Michael said, the word like a knife slashing down.

Eryn recoiled, squeezing against the passenger-side door. She heard Nick slide over in the back, too.

"Sorry," Michael said. "I just . . ." He swallowed hard and seemed to be gritting his teeth. When he spoke again, it was in a calmer tone. "I'll explain. It's very difficult to build a robot that can mimic all the growth and changes a typical human child makes between birth and adulthood. Some would say it's impossible. So the people who set up Project Return of the Snowflakes didn't even try. But they didn't want you and the others your age to wonder why there weren't any kids older than you. So they provided for . . . facsimile robot children . . . that could stay a certain age as long as they were needed. Placeholders that could be easily destroyed."

He said the last word like a curse. It froze Eryn in place.

"The year both of you turned one," Michael continued, staring straight ahead, "all the toddler robot children were melted down for scrap. The year you turned two, the same thing happened to the two-year-old robots. And so on, and so on, day by day and month by month, robot children being destroyed as soon as the earliest human children reached their particular ages. All the robots who were created to be precisely twelve years old are gone now. So are the ones who were twelve years old and one day. And the ones who were twelve years old and two days. You see how it works? It won't be long before they start destroying the thirteen-year-olds. And then the fourteen-year-olds . . . There's no age we could claim for Ava and Jackson that wouldn't make them either illegal—or slated for destruction."

Eryn couldn't let herself think that word—*destruction*—in connection with Ava and Jackson. Kids she'd been wondering about for months. Her thoughts darted to Milo, the boy who'd invited her and Nick to go sledding. The first robot kid she'd ever met that she'd known was a robot.

He was probably thirteen. Probably about to be destroyed.

"That can't be true!" she argued, facing Michael

again. "You've got to be lying! We'd notice if kids just a year ahead of us were constantly disappearing!"

"You probably think you'd notice older kids staying the same age for years on end, too," Michael said, with a bitter twist to his words. "But think about it. Tell me the name of one kid a grade ahead of you that you've known your entire childhood. Or *any* older kid you stayed in contact with for much longer than a year."

"Well, there's . . . ," Eryn began. There had to be somebody. But she came up with a blank.

She turned to Nick for help. He had his hand over his mouth, his face twisted in a grimace.

"Uh, Eryn, he might be right," Nick said slowly, letting his hand slip. "Doesn't it seem like the older kids we played with were always moving out of the neighborhood? Or Mom decided they were bad influences and we couldn't play with them anymore, or their parents sent them away to their grandparents or to some kind of boarding school, or . . ."

"Or we're just classic first-borns, like Mom's always telling us, and we tend to play with younger kids so we can be in charge," Eryn said. "That doesn't prove anything!"

The car skidded a little on black ice, and Michael

slowed down even more. The slight jarring must have done something to Eryn's brain. Awakened it a little.

"Oh, we're idiots!" Eryn said. "What about *Mom*? She's a *middle* school psychologist—she deals with teenagers all the time. *Real* teenagers, not robots. I knew this whole story couldn't be true!"

Now she just needed something to make herself un-see the wires hanging out of Mom's stomach, un-see the ones hanging out of Michael's ex-wife's stomach, un-see the entire cyber-innards of Ava and Jackson. . . .

Eryn gave up trying to make herself see the world as normal again.

Also, Michael *wasn't* grinning and saying *Oh, right. You caught me. You found the gaping hole in my story.*

"Your mother has been *practicing* on robot teenagers for the past twelve years," Michael said calmly. "The same seventh, eighth, and ninth graders every single year. I have to tell you, she's terrified of next year, when she'll have to deal with human teens. From everything she's read, human teenagers are much less . . . predictable . . . than the robot version."

Michael was just inching the car forward. It made Eryn want to scream.

"But I'll tell you, the robot babies and toddlers were

every bit as cute as the human versions," Michael said, with an ache in his voice. "The kindergarteners were just as gap-toothed and inquisitive as human kindergarteners. The third-grade robots were just as proud of knowing their times tables. The—"

"Stop it!" Eryn snapped.

Michael shook his head, like he couldn't stop.

"Now they're all gone," he finished, even as he stared bleakly out the windshield.

"You make it sound like genocide or something," Nick complained, leaning all the way forward so his head was practically in between Eryn's and Michael's. "Like what those bad guys—the Nazis?—did in the last century. I mean, the twentieth century. Whatever. But about destroying the robot children—you robots are the ones doing that yourselves, right? It's your own fault!"

Michael clutched the steering wheel so hard his knuckles turned white.

"It's how we were programmed," he said tightly. "And . . . as you and your contemporaries grow to adulthood and beyond, eventually all the robots will be gone. Because just as you and your fellow humans became the only five-year-olds, the only eight-year-olds, the only eleven-year-olds, eventually you'll be all the fifty-year-olds, all the eighty-year-olds, all the adults. *That's* what 'fully human society' means. No more robots."

Eryn thought about that. Mom and Dad, gone? All the other grown-ups gone too?

Of course, she'd always known that everyone died eventually, but this seemed worse somehow. Everyone *like* Mom and Dad would be gone.

"Oh, come on," Eryn said, and somehow the words came out sounding more sarcastic than she intended. "I bet you just misunderstood. In the video they said the humans were in danger of going extinct, and there wasn't much time to make all the arrangements, so of course what they focused on was making sure the human embryos survived. They probably wouldn't mind if robots continued too . . . somewhere."

Even to Eryn's ears, that sounded like a lame argument. But Michael smiled as if he loved every word she spoke.

"That," he said, "is exactly why I created Ava and Jackson. Or, I should say, arranged for my ex-wife Brenda to give birth to them."

"Oh," Nick said. Eryn heard him thump back against his seat, as if he didn't have the energy to absorb another surprise.

Michael glanced in the rearview mirror and kept smiling.

"Our entire robot society was created with the intent of raising and nurturing children," he said. "It was such a paradox of our programming that we were designed for parenthood but we were never allowed to raise children of our own, robots like us—not all the way from birth to adulthood, anyway. The only robot children any of us were allowed had to stay stuck at the same age their entire lives. And then be destroyed so young . . ."

Don't you count us *as your own children?* Eryn wanted to ask. But she kept silent. Even with Michael driving slowly, they were almost to Lipman Park. They had only a little longer to hear Michael's story.

"So a few of us got together, way back at the beginning," Michael said. "Your parents were in that group from the start. Your mom contributed psychological insights; your father had more of the mechanical skills. And I was the lead programmer. We began experimenting with ways to make robot children who could grow up from birth on, normally and naturally."

What's normal or natural about a robot? Eryn thought.

But again, she didn't say anything, and neither did Nick.

"We knew our actions could be seen as treason by the wider society, but we were determined," Michael continued. "We were certain that once we proved it was possible, we could convince everyone else we had the right idea. Then, we thought, we could modify the original plans, and eventually there would be generations of robots raising robot children right next door to humans raising human children. . . . We had to operate in secret, but everything was going so well."

"Was?" Nick asked faintly from the backseat.

"When Ava and Jackson hit adolescence, all their programming fell apart," Michael said, and now his smile vanished. "We'd been able to pass them off as human before that—they were even going to a regular school! We'd hacked into all sorts of listings to make that possible. We thought this year would be the point when we could test the kids' ability to seem human around the clock, and even live with stepsiblings—with you! Ava and Jackson, they're *why* your mom and I got married."

Oh, how romantic of you, Eryn thought, feeling hurt on Mom's behalf.

But what did she expect? Mom and Michael were robots.

"We'd already checked into getting a marriage license," Michael said. "We'd told our bosses. We were . . . publicly committed to a certain path. Then, right before we told you kids, everything with Ava and Jackson started going wrong. Now we can't even let them out of the house. We have to keep them a bigger secret than ever."

The tense way he said that made Eryn's stomach hurt.

"You have a soundproofed car," Nick said, still speaking softly. That wasn't like him. Eryn couldn't tell if he was terrified or traumatized. Or both. "You say it even protects against lip-reading. But what good does any of that do? Couldn't a robot have supersonic hearing? Or X-ray vision? Mom acted like someone might hear us inside our own house!"

"We're being extra, extra cautious," Michael said. "Robots aren't supposed to have any better sight or hearing than normal human beings. But what if somebody's breaking those rules the way we're breaking the rule about robotic children? And . . . robots do have ways of keeping track of each other that humans don't have.

Think of it as being like how computers are linked on the Internet. We can keep some things private, but . . ."

But there are computer hackers, Eryn thought. *Like you.*

Were there robot-brain hackers, too?

Eryn didn't want to ask that question. But she remembered how Milo and the other neighborhood sledders had shown up so quickly after Nick and Eryn found out Mom was a robot.

"Michael, what if your secret's already out?" she gasped. She saw Michael tense beside her. "These kids from our neighborhood—older, *robot* kids—they showed up at our door to test us, like, right after we started asking questions about Ava and Jackson. It was like someone had called them."

Michael slumped down again and let out a sigh.

"You scared me there for a minute," he said. "That's not a sign of any problem—your mother was the one who summoned those kids. Indirectly. She sent out an alert that it was time for the first viewing of the video, and part of that protocol is for the child or children in question to be tested. To see if they can be trusted not to tell other kids everything they know."

"Oh," Eryn said.

Michael may have been more relaxed now, but somehow she didn't feel any better.

"So it's like there are really two big secrets we know now," Nick said. "One about the extinction and the robots and the whole Project Snowflake, which we're not allowed to talk about with any other humans. Not until the other kids are ready and see the video themselves. And the other secret is about Ava and Jackson, which we're not allowed to tell anyone."

"Exactly," Michael said.

For a moment, it was quiet in the dark car. Eryn let herself think only about Ava and Jackson. Their secret felt tiny—even minor—compared with frozen embryos and human extinction and some unknown threat off in the future. Eryn let out a small half-giggle. If Mom and Michael had gone through with their plan to throw Ava and Jackson into a stepsibling relationship with Nick and Eryn, that truly would have tested their ability to act like real human beings.

At least I won't have to deal with that *anytime soon,* Eryn thought. *Thank you, Ava and Jackson's screwy programming.*

"So when—" she started to ask, but just then Michael stopped the car. Eryn had gotten so engrossed in his story that she hadn't looked out the window for several blocks, hadn't kept track at all of where they were. How could they be home already?

Eryn rubbed a little hole in the fog that had built up on the car window.

They weren't home. They were at Ava and Jackson's house.

THIRTY-FOUR

"Why are we here?" Eryn asked.

So Eryn's capable of asking deep, philosophical questions, Nick thought. *Even if Mom and Dad couldn't teach us about philosophy.*

Then he looked out the window and realized she wasn't asking about their purpose in life.

"This is a good time for you to meet Ava and Jackson," Michael said. "For real."

Because we're too tired to argue? Nick thought. *Because we've seen and heard so many strange things today, we'd barely notice one or two more?*

Neither he nor Eryn moved.

"This house has soundproofing too," Michael said, as if that was supposed to be a comforting thought. "So you don't have to worry about anything bad happening."

Michael thinks the worst thing that could happen

is someone overhearing us? Nick wondered. *Um, what about extinction? What about . . .*

Nick couldn't let himself keep thinking of potential disasters, or he'd never move.

"We are still curious about Ava and Jackson," Eryn said, but she didn't sound curious. She sounded pummeled, squashed flat, practically defeated.

Nick made himself reach for the door handle.

"Just don't say anything . . . incriminating . . . between the car and the house," Michael said. "We won't have soundproofing there."

Oh, that's helpful, Nick thought. *Thanks for scaring us even more.*

But Michael's warning woke up Nick's curiosity again. Who could possibly be listening on a quiet residential street, on a night when all the neighbors would have their houses shut up tight against the cold? Were Michael and his ex-wife—and, Nick guessed, Mom and Dad too—really in that much danger of being caught? Or were they just being paranoid? Why was it so wrong to have robot children who grew up, anyway?

What were Ava and Jackson like when they weren't malfunctioning?

Nick opened the door and got out. The brutal wind was a shock against his face after the warm car, but he made himself walk toward the house. Eryn and Michael joined him, a few steps behind.

Michael's ex-wife already had the front door open, bracing it against the wind.

"Welcome," she called out into the darkness. "Welcome. We are so happy to see you!"

She was beaming as if that were true. As if the whole reason she existed was to meet Nick and Eryn.

Which, if you thought about it, was kind of true.

Nick stumbled across the threshold, his boots feeling particularly heavy on his feet.

"Sorry," he muttered. "I'm tracking in snow. . . ."

He bent down to untie his boots, but Michael's ex-wife patted him on the back.

"Oh, don't worry about it," she said heartily. "I know how to use a mop. So do Ava and Jackson!"

The way her eyes twinkled—was that some robot trick to make people like her?

She flipped a strand of wavy red hair over her shoulder and turned to engulf Eryn in a huge hug.

She's like Mrs. Galloway, my kindergarten teacher, Nick thought. *She's like . . . radiant.*

Mrs. Galloway had been a grandmotherly woman who wore aprons when they were fingerpainting or making play-dough out of salt and flour. Michael's ex-wife was a lot younger, and, well, prettier. But she had the same air of making you feel like you were the most special person alive.

Now it struck Nick, belatedly, *Wait a minute. Even Mrs. Galloway wasn't human? Even* she *was a robot?*

That seemed impossible. Unbelievable. Mrs. Galloway had been like the real live human version of Mrs. Santa Claus.

Except . . . not, Nick told himself. *Not actually human. She was just programmed that way.*

Would shocks like this keep hitting him the rest of his life, as he kept figuring everything out?

"Oh please, call me Brenda," Michael's ex-wife said, and Nick guessed he'd missed Eryn stammering out, "Oh, hello, Mrs., uh . . ."

Michael kissed Brenda on the cheek, the exact same way Dad always kissed Mom. Nick's brain kicked up a rebellious thought: *Well, of course it's exactly the same. They're all robots. Everything they do is robotic. I just never knew that before.*

Brenda shut the door behind Michael and leaned to the side to call up the stairs, "Hey, kids! Dad and Nick and Eryn are here!"

Ava and Jackson must have been waiting at the top of

the stairs, because they came clattering down the steps immediately.

"Sorry my brain wasn't working right before," Jackson said, giving Nick a friendly kid-to-kid slug on the arm. "Now I remember everything about you. It's really great to see you guys again!"

Jackson looked like a normal kid now, maybe even better than normal: shiny hair, smooth skin, casual smile. . . . If he'd been in Nick's class at school, Jackson would have been one of those guys the sixth-grade girls acted silly over, giggling and stammering and blushing whenever he was near. (This had happened a couple of times to Nick himself, and Eryn had punched him in the arm and said, "Get over yourself. Some girls are so desperate to fall in love, they'll fall in love with *anyone.*" He was pretty sure she was quoting Mom.) Nick had to remind himself he'd seen wires and circuits inside Jackson's body; he'd seen that under his skin, Jackson was nothing *but* wires and circuitry.

"This is so sick, getting to meet you," Ava chimed in. "Do kids at your school say *sick*, when they mean something is really, really great? Kids did that at our old school, before we started the homeschooling."

She was doing what Eryn did sometimes when she was nervous, chattering away about nothing.

But Ava's doing it robotically, Nick reminded himself. *Because she's a robot.*

"Why don't we all sit down?" Brenda said, gesturing toward the living room. Nick could see that all the window blinds were pulled all the way down now. So no one would be able to see in.

"Ava and Jackson made oatmeal cookies this afternoon, and we just put a plateful on the coffee table," Brenda continued. "There's hot cocoa, too—seems like a perfect night for it, don't you think?"

Michael nudged Nick and Eryn toward the nearest couch, but he said, "Oh, we can't stay long. Nick and Eryn haven't even had dinner yet. Those cookies look delicious, but—kids, please don't eat too many. Don't ruin your appetite."

Nick sat down and took a cookie, and it was exactly the way he liked: warm and melty, full of chocolate chips and raisins. But his first bite stuck in his throat, and he didn't think washing it down with cocoa would help.

"We made some of the cookies without raisins, too," Ava said, making more nervous chatter. "Because not everybody likes raisins. But I've never met anyone who didn't like chocolate chips."

"Some people are allergic," Jackson said.

"That's *tragic*," Ava said, grinning in a way that made fun of herself. As if she were trying to get Nick and Eryn to laugh.

"Is anybody ever allergic to oatmeal?" Nick asked, because it was easier to talk about food than all the weird thoughts and questions bouncing around in his head. "I mean, I like oatmeal, but why aren't people very often allergic to things that are good for them? Like brussels sprouts. Is anyone ever allergic to brussels sprouts?"

"Or liver," Jackson said with a shudder.

Nick could talk about food all night.

"Or—" he began.

He realized that Eryn hadn't sat down with the rest of them. She hadn't taken a cookie or picked up the mug of cocoa Brenda poured for her. Eryn was still standing in the foyer, her arms crossed, her feet planted firmly in what Mom always called *Eryn's stubborn stance*.

"Why are we pretending?" Eryn asked. She narrowed her eyes and peered at Michael. Her gaze might as well have been laser-focused. "What were you trying to accomplish, bringing Nick and me here tonight?"

"I—" Michael began helplessly. "We—"

Brenda stood up and went to stand behind him. She

put her hand on his shoulder, the motion very deliberate and precise.

Divorced couple trick, Nick thought.

Mom and Dad had moves like that, little gestures that all but spoke aloud, *We may not be married anymore, but we are completely united on this issue.*

"We wanted you to see how lovable Ava and Jackson really are," Brenda said. "Or at least, how much we love them."

"You have to know what could be destroyed if you make any mistakes," Michael added. He crossed his arm over his heart to put his hand on his ex-wife's, which still rested on his shoulder. "Our children's lives depend on you keeping their secret."

"*Our* lives depend on you keeping the secret too," Brenda said. "So do your parents'."

But none of you are actually alive, *are you?* Nick thought rebelliously. *You're just . . . fully charged. Functioning. Running smoothly. Adequately designed.*

He was tempted to say this out loud; maybe Eryn would say something like it.

But just then Ava began to cry. Tears trembled in her eyelashes just as if she were a real girl.

"Please . . . ," she whispered.

Jackson patted his sister's arm. His hair was mussed in the same way Nick's hair always got mussed. He had a little smear of chocolate at the corner of his mouth. He didn't look so perfect anymore.

He just looked human. Completely human.

"Please don't let us die," he said.

THIRTY-FIVE

We're all in danger, Eryn thought.

It felt like the craziest thought ever. She was sitting in her second-period social studies class the morning after the snow day, and the room was so peaceful and still she could hear the scratch of Angelina Biddle's pencil on her "Map of the United States" worksheet two rows over. First period, everyone had excitedly chattered about what they'd done on their day off—well, everyone except Nick and Eryn had. But now the whole class had settled into the usual routine. Mr. Carrera taught a lesson; he gave the class an assignment; the class did it. Even Eryn herself was absentmindedly coloring in the outlined states—green for Colorado, blue for Kansas, red for Nebraska. . . . The routine felt like a weight on her shoulders, holding her down, keeping her in her seat even as she longed to jump up and shout at everyone, *Do any of you know what's really going on? Did you ever notice all the adults are robots? Do you know we're all in danger of going extinct—again?*

Of course, it wasn't just the routine that held her down. It was also the fear that if she started talking, she wouldn't be able to stop, and she'd reveal too much. Saying *anything* would be too much, she guessed—she had promised to let all the other human children find out about Project Return of the Snowflakes at their own pace. And she was certain that every other kid in her class was human—she'd looked at their eyes to be sure. But what if she said something about Ava and Jackson that got Mom and Michael in trouble? Would Mom and Michael be taken away and thrown into prison? Would they be killed? (*Shut down,* her brain corrected. *Melted down for scrap. Recycled.*) Dad and Brenda would be taken away too; Ava and Jackson would almost certainly be destroyed.

Then what would happen to Nick and Eryn? Would someone adopt them? Would they be thrown into prison themselves? Or a mental hospital?

Someone tells you your entire species is in danger of extinction, and all you care about is what's going to happen to you and your family? Eryn scolded herself. *When three-fourths of them aren't even human anyway?*

Eryn put down her red pencil and rubbed her eyes, like she was still trying to erase everything she'd seen yesterday. If she hadn't seen the wires and circuits and motherboards inside (or hanging out of) Ava, Jackson, Brenda, and Mom, she wouldn't have believed a single word anyone said about robots or danger, human snowflakes or human extinction.

Eryn realized she was rubbing her eyes little-kid style: her hands balled into fists, rotating back and forth. This made her think of a game Mom had always tried to get her to play when she was little. Eryn had been a tantrum-thrower, and when Eryn cried and screamed inconsolably over dropped ice cream cones or stubbed toes or broken crayons, Mom would crouch down beside her and whisper, "Explain with words, not screams. What happened? How did that make you feel?"

I feel . . . mad, Eryn thought now, and she was so surprised she stopped rubbing her eyes and just sat there. Now she probably looked like someone pretending her fists were binoculars, enabling her to look far off into the distance. That was okay for kindergartners, but it was the kind of thing that would get a sixth-grader labeled weird.

Normally Eryn tried very hard not to get labeled

weird, but she kept her hands right where they were.

Are *you mad?* She asked herself.

She was.

Buried under all the surprise and confusion and fear, she felt a huge, roiling lake of fury inside herself. Where Jackson's innards were entirely taken up with wires and circuitry, hers seemed to be nothing but rage.

She was mad at Mom and Michael for thinking Nick and Eryn could accept secret, hidden stepsiblings without question, without snooping.

She was mad at Michael and Brenda (and Mom and Dad and whoever else was involved) for breaking the law and creating Ava and Jackson in the first place.

She was mad at Mom for not telling them everything immediately, on the phone, the very first moment Eryn and Nick confessed they'd seen Jackson and Ava.

She was mad at Mom and Dad for getting divorced when they really didn't have to.

She was mad at Mom and the mayor for not spelling out exactly what would happen to Nick and Eryn if they ever told any other human about Project Snowflakes. Even if they just slipped up and did it by accident.

She was mad at the two people in the videotape—Dr. Grimaldi and Dr. Speck—for not explaining what caused the extinction the first time around and what Eryn and Nick and the other Snowflakes needed to do to prevent humanity from ending forever.

I was raised by robots, Eryn thought. *I expect logic. I expect to-do lists.*

She was mad at the last generation of humans before hers for not stopping their own extinction their own stupid selves.

But most of all, she was mad at herself and Nick.

Why did we agree to leave City Hall before we had all our questions answered? she wondered. *Why did we let Michael sidetrack us with Ava and Jackson? Why didn't we stay up all night asking questions? Why did we let Mom tuck us into bed like usual? Why did we let her pretend everything was normal this morning, and send us off to school like usual? Why am I sitting in social studies doing a worksheet that isn't even going to be graded when, for all I know, every second counts? When we could be on the brink of extinction and past the point of no return at any moment?*

Eryn knew the answers to those questions. She and Nick had been shocked and confused and scared—and they still were. It'd been the easiest thing in the world to go back to their usual routine and pretend nothing had changed. It would be the easiest thing in the world to go on pretending forever.

But I can't keep pretending, Eryn thought. *Not the rest of my life. Not even the rest of this class.*

Eryn took her hands off her face, uncovering her eyes.

And then she stood up.

THIRTY-SIX

Nick had been as jumpy as a cat all morning. The kid next to him, Evan Nondingo, snapped the lead on his pencil, and Nick practically leaped out of his skin. The girl in front of him, Ivy Mahalo, flipped her long hair over her shoulder so the tips of it brushed Nick's hand, and Nick jerked away so forcefully that his chair went momentarily airborne, landing three inches back.

Then Nick saw Eryn stand up, and he practically fell to the floor.

"Eryn, no," he cried, his voice booming out in the quiet classroom. "Don't—"

Don't tell anyone anything, he wanted to say. *Don't do anything to call attention to yourself.*

But Nick was the one everyone turned to stare at. Everyone probably thought he was acting even weirder than Eryn.

"I think my sister's sick," Nick said apologetically.

"She might even be delirious. She might start saying a bunch of crazy stuff you can't believe."

The other kids just stared more, with wider eyes. Nick could tell they were thinking, *First a snow day, and now this. Drama! Excitement! Wait till we tell the other kids in the school!*

At the front of the room, Mr. Carrera scowled suspiciously, his dark eyebrows mashing together.

"Eryn?" he said. "This is work-on-your-worksheet time. You did not have permission to stand. You are causing a disruption and interrupting the entire class. What do you have to say for yourself?"

Only a robot teacher could sound that calm, Nick thought.

Why hadn't he and Eryn and all the other kids noticed before?

Because we always thought that's just how teachers are, Nick told himself. *That's how all the grown-ups act.*

Trying to figure that out made him miss the chance to stop Eryn from answering. It was too late for even the most drastic effort. There wasn't time to spring up from his seat at the back of the room and tackle her and use his hand as a gag over her mouth.

"I need to speak to my mother," Eryn said.

Of all the things she might have said, that wasn't too bad. She sounded calmer and less crazy than Nick.

But maybe she was just warming up.

"You know we have begun letting students use their cell phones at lunchtime," Mr. Carrera said mildly. "Perhaps you can text your mother then."

"I need to speak to her right now," Eryn said. Her voice was still calm and controlled, but it got steelier with every word she spoke.

Nick knew his sister. When she got like this, nobody could stop her.

Nick bolted from his seat. In his haste, he forgot how much he'd grown since the beginning of the school year, and how the desk was just a little too small for him now. His leg slammed against the desk's leg, and he imagined himself sprinting down the aisle toward Eryn with the desk around his ankle; he'd be like an escaped prisoner dragging along his chains.

But Nick didn't stop or even slow down. Maybe he was just as stubborn as Eryn.

He did shake his leg a little, disengaging from the desk.

"I'll take my sister to the school nurse," Nick volunteered. "I'll make sure she's all right."

Mr. Carrera's eyes constricted slightly. It was such a mechanized movement it made Nick wonder if the man—er, robot—had some way of mentally calling up Nick's and Eryn's behavior records dating all the way back to kindergarten. Maybe even preschool. Robots were essentially computers in human form, weren't they? And Michael had said robots were linked kind of like the Internet. So couldn't Mr. Carrera have something like Google Glass even when he wasn't actually wearing glasses?

Stop thinking about stuff like that, Nick told himself. *You'll freak yourself out and just freeze. Focus on rescuing Eryn from making an even bigger mistake.*

Mr. Carrera seemed to be deciding Nick could be trusted. His eyebrows relaxed; his eyes went back to normal.

Or what if he already knows what Eryn and I found out last night? Nick wondered. *What if he's decided Eryn and I need to be quarantined from the other kids?*

Maybe Mr. Carrera and the rest of the teachers would decide Nick and Eryn had to be to be homeschooled like Ava and Jackson. Maybe they'd be kept locked in their rooms to study.

That would be awful.

Nick was so busy imagining what could go wrong, he almost missed hearing Mr. Carrera say resignedly, "Yes, Nick, you may take Eryn to the nurse. That is far preferable to having the two of you continue to disrupt class."

"Thank you," Eryn said, drawing out the words as if she and Mr. Carrera had been facing off in a fight, and she'd just won.

Nick grabbed Eryn's arm and dragged her toward the door. She walked alongside him, but acted like he wasn't there. She didn't even glance his way until they were out in the hallway and far enough away from Mr. Carrera's room that nobody would hear them.

None of the other kids would, anyway. If Mom and Michael were paranoid about being overheard in their own home or car or driveway, who knew who might be listening in the school?

"What did you think I was going to do?" Eryn finally asked. She sounded offended.

"What *are* you doing?" Nick asked.

Eryn didn't answer right away. Her footsteps echoed too loudly in the silent hallway. This just wasn't normal. Nobody left the classroom in the middle of class unless it was an emergency. You had to be vomiting or gushing blood or . . .

In danger of extinction? Nick thought.

He gulped, and his hand slipped off Eryn's arm. That was the revelation he'd heard last night that he was having the most trouble thinking about. So he didn't. He wouldn't.

But maybe he had to?

"I'm going to tell Mom she has to come and pick us up," Eryn said. "And then we're going to go see the president of the United States."

THIRTY-SEVEN

"The . . . president?" Nick repeated numbly, and his eyelids sprang wide open. His pupils stayed big and dark; he looked like someone who'd just had a concussion. Or was still in shock. "Why would the president talk to us?"

"Because of what we found out," Eryn said impatiently. "Because we're the first kids to know anything, and we need to know more than the mayor or anyone else around here can tell us. A little bit of knowledge is a dangerous thing." She thought maybe that was a quote. "It doesn't *have* to be the president. Just someone who knows the truth. Someone who can tell us . . ."

"Why people went extinct before and what we can do to stop it now," Nick finished for her. She was torn between wanting to hug him for finally catching on, and wanting to shove him behind her to protect him if he was going to get in trouble for saying those words aloud, out in public.

But there aren't any other kids nearby, and it's only kids we have to worry about hearing that particular secret, she reminded herself. *Only human kids.*

There wasn't a single other person—or robot—in sight. The school hallway was silent and still, except for the sound of their own shoes against the hard tile floor.

Eryn stopped walking.

"The nurse is just going to ask questions," she said. "Do you think it's safe to stop right here and call Mom?"

They were in the long stretch of hallway without classrooms. The school library was on one side, and they could see nothing through its windows but the soaring shelves of books. The gymnasium was on the other side, and it must have been the P.E. teacher's open period, because Eryn couldn't hear even the muffled thud of basketballs hitting the wall.

Nick responded by grabbing Eryn's arm again and pulling her down to the floor.

"If anybody asks, I can say you got really sick," he told her. "Too sick to go on."

Is he a little too good at coming up with lies and excuses? Eryn wondered.

But she let Nick tug her down to sit on the floor. She pulled out her phone and dialed.

Mom answered instantly, which made Eryn think that Mom also must have been having trouble sticking with her usual routine—her usual pretense.

"What's wrong?" Mom said.

Normally, Mom would never start a conversation like that. Now it was almost becoming a habit.

"Everything's fine," Eryn said, as if she was the grown-up and Mom was the kid who needed comforting. "It's just, we have to have more answers. You know it's human nature to be curious."

Did Mom know that? Did she really understand, or was it just some rote thing she'd repeated to the kids because she was supposed to: *Human beings are curious. It's perfectly normal and natural for you to feel this way.*

"You need more answers about . . . ," Mom prompted cautiously.

"She's afraid it's . . . you know," Nick whispered. He had his head pressed against Eryn's so he could hear Mom too.

Eryn knew he meant Ava and Jackson. The secret they weren't allowed to tell anyone.

"Answers about . . . the extinction," Eryn said. She found that her hand was trembling. She braced the phone against her head to stop it. "We have to know how to stop it from happening again."

"I understand you have a desire for more information," Mom said. And this was her school psychologist voice, her reflective listening trick—which always made Eryn mad.

"It's not about you understanding me, Mom," Eryn said, and now she kind of wished for bouncing basketballs in the gymnasium, to cover the sound of her own voice. She was getting a little screechy. She kept talking anyway. "It's about action. We *have* to find out. We have to do whatever it takes. Take us to the governor or the president or—"

"That wouldn't do any good," Mom interrupted, still in her most calming voice. "The governor and the president don't know what caused the extinction either."

Then why are they the governor and the president? Eryn wondered. *How could our elected officials be so stupid?*

"Okay, never mind them," she said abruptly. Because right now, they didn't matter. "Take us to whoever *does* know. I don't care how far we have to go—we have to find out!"

"Oh, Eryn," Mom said, and she sounded truly sad,

truly apologetic. Even if she was just a robot. "It's not that I don't want to help you through this difficult time of revelation. It's not that I want to frustrate you in your very human quest for truth. It's just—"

"Just what?" Eryn asked, exasperated. She realized that Nick had chimed in, speaking the words with her.

"Just that nobody can help you," Mom finished. "Because nobody knows what caused the extinction."

THIRTY-EIGHT

"How do you know nobody knows?" Nick asked.

Mom had come to pick them up from school, and now they were driving home. On the phone, she'd told them she'd explain later; at least she hadn't made them wait until the end of the day. Instead, she'd given their school a flimsy-sounding excuse about them being out in the cold too much the day before and needing to "rest." Nobody questioned it.

Because they're robots, Nick thought. *The principal, the vice principal, the school secretary, the school nurse . . .*

He realized Mom hadn't answered his question. He repeated it, leaning forward so he could poke his head over the back of Mom's seat.

"And really," Eryn added, hitting the dashboard as if she'd just figured something out, "how do you know the president and the governor and maybe even the mayor don't keep lots of secrets from you? How do you know there isn't lots of information they say they don't know but really it's just top secret or classified or . . ."

Mom sighed.

"They're public officials," she said. "Every citizen has the right to examine all of their memory banks, all of their programming . . ."

"You can read their minds?" Nick exclaimed. "Anytime you want?"

Mom seemed to be gritting her teeth.

"That's one way to put it," she admitted. Now she seemed to be concentrating very hard on steering the car. She acted like she might need to turn on a dime. "Michael said he told you how robots can connect, kind of like the Internet. Let's just say . . . you know how you might use your phone to connect wirelessly to the Internet just about anywhere, anytime? We can do that too, to access certain public information. We just . . . don't need to use phones."

We, Nick realized, were all the grown-ups. All the robots.

So he had been right to think that Mr. Carrera had something like Google Glass without actually wearing it.

"Is it public information that Nick and I saw the video?" Eryn asked. "That we *know*?"

Mom was silent for a moment. Then she said, very softly, "Yes."

We're famous! Nick thought. *Everyone thinks Eryn and I are brilliant!*

He looked out the window, and even though they were driving down a quiet residential street, he suddenly felt like there might be a million eyes watching him.

Maybe it wasn't such a good thing to be famous. Especially when they were supposed to be keeping an illegal secret, too.

"So, this connection between robots . . . is that how the school officials knew not to ask questions when you came to pick us up today?" Nick said. He had to know how much the robots knew. "Is that how Mr. Carrera knew he had to let Eryn and me leave class? Is that how you knew I broke the window at Teddy Vickers's eighth birthday party even before his mom told you? Is that why you and Dad never seem surprised by anything we tell you that happened at the other parent's house . . . ?"

Once he got started, he could think of so many instances to ask about. But Mom put her hand out to stop him.

"You're bringing up too many different cases," she complained. "The first two examples—yes, those are from the public connections. But the others, those are just from parents conferring privately. Parents sharing necessary information, which other adults are required to provide from their own memory banks upon request."

Nick saw Eryn's jaw drop.

"But we always try to model responsible verbal communication in front of you," Mom went on, pursing her lips primly. "We do talk, too. Because when your generation grows up, you won't have the advantage of—"

"Constant spying?" Eryn exploded. "You're trying to tell us that every adult can find out anything every other adult knows, if they really want to? Every adult can see and hear anything any adult has seen or heard? Then how in the world could *anyone* keep a secret? Any adult, I mean—any robot. How did Michael and the rest of you ever think you could keep it a secret when—"

Nick knew her next words were going to be about Ava and Jackson. Mom seemed to know it too, because all of a sudden, she slammed her hand against the horn. The blaring sound made Nick jump, and Eryn gasped rather than saying another word.

"Oh dear," Mom said, a bit too loudly. "My eyes must be playing tricks on me. Didn't that snowdrift at the side of the road look just like a goose that was about to step out in front of the car?"

The snowdrift at the side of the road just looked like snow. Nobody could have imagined it was a goose.

Mom isn't saying that for our benefit, Nick thought. *She's trying to make it seem like she had a reason for honking the horn just then, besides wanting to keep Eryn from finishing her sentence. Mom thinks someone might be listening. Or will listen to the conversation in the future. Maybe even the way it sounds through her own ears?*

This thought totally creeped him out.

Mom turned toward Eryn.

"Honey, I know you're trying to understand a lot of complicated information, but you've got to wait for me to explain before you start making wild accusations," Mom said. "Public officials are the only ones who are required to make *all* their thoughts and memories publicly accessible. Everyone else can shut off certain segments of their memory banks if they wish. And if it's reasonable. Because humans value privacy. We need to model that for you as well."

Nick guessed that was her way of telling Eryn how Michael and the others had managed to keep the truth about Ava and Jackson secret for the past twelve years.

"So then, couldn't someone who isn't a public official

know what made humans extinct?" Eryn asked. Nick was impressed at how she could shift an argument back to what she wanted to know. Even if he himself felt a little queasy about finding out anything.

"And then," Eryn continued, "couldn't that person just keep that information in his secret memory banks? You can't have it both ways. Either people can keep secrets or they can't."

"They can, but not if someone sends out an all-call begging for facts," Mom said. "Then they're required to reveal even secret information. They can't resist that call—not without violating their programming. And I just made a call like that. I just asked every person on the entire planet to tell me if they knew anything about what made humans extinct. And every person on the planet said no."

"By *person*, you mean *robot*, right?" Eryn asked in her snarliest voice.

Mom winced.

"Yes," she said quietly. "Some people sent in their speculation about what might have happened—climate scientists concerned about human effects on the environment, peace activists theorizing about nuclear war, epidemiologists worried about the worst plague ever, or weaponized Ebola virus, or something like that. When we get home I'll download their ideas onto your laptops, and you can look through them if you want."

Mom went back to looking straight out the windshield and driving carefully. Eryn turned around and peered at Nick. Her eyes were narrowed into her most extreme squint ever. Nick could tell she was trying to send the message, *Isn't this insane? How could it be that no one knows what made every human being on the planet die? How can we believe anything Mom tells us? She's got to be lying!*

Looking back at Eryn, Nick opened his eyes as wide as he could. This probably made him look scared, but he didn't care. Because what he wanted to say to Eryn was, *I'm not so sure. What does it mean if she's actually telling the truth?*

THIRTY-NINE

Eryn hated computer research.

If she needed to find out something, she always tried every other source she could think of before opening her laptop. One time for school she'd mixed an entire bottle of vinegar with an entire carton of baking soda and watched it explode—and then had to clean up the mess afterward—rather than watching a single video of someone else doing the same experiment.

But now here she was, staring at tiny print on the computer screen. Nick sat beside her on the couch, peering at his own laptop.

Mom had disappeared into her bedroom.

"You have to understand, this is upsetting to me as well," Mom had explained. "It is perfectly valid that you wish to make this exploration. But it is also perfectly natural that I feel slightly rejected, that your quest for information beyond what I possess feels like a judgment of my adequacy as a parent. . . ."

Eryn had had to bite her tongue not to snarl back, *Mom, you're a robot! You can't feel anything! You're just pretending!*

Now she bent her head lower over the computer screen. Phrases leaped out at her, the theories robots from around the world had come up with for why humans had originally gone extinct: "excessive carbon emissions . . . ," "overpopulation and depletion of resources . . . ," "air pollution and irreversible destruction of human lung tissue . . . ," "global pandemic . . . ," "viral mutation . . . ," "warring nations and mutually assured destruction . . . ," "natural disasters such as volcanic eruption . . ."

"We're just kids," Eryn said despairingly. "How are we supposed to know which theory is right? How would anybody know?"

Nick glanced up from his own laptop. He'd been absentmindedly running his fingers through his hair as he read, so his dark hair stuck up almost as messily as Dad's always did.

Nick's going to look just like Dad when he grows up, Eryn thought. *He definitely got all his genes from Dad's side.*

Then she remembered that Nick had come from a frozen embryo, and Dad was just a robot. He didn't even have genes to pass down to Nick.

Ugh, ugh, ugh, Eryn thought. *They probably designed Dad and Mom to look like they were genetically related to us, just so we wouldn't ask questions. . . .*

She realized she was missing Nick's answer.

"Huh?" she said.

"Haven't you gotten to this part yet?" Nick asked, pointing to something on his screen. "Where they explain that there are scientific tests people could do to find out about some of these hypotheses—like looking for volcanic ash in glaciers in Antarctica, or digging up corpses and doing autopsies."

Eryn fiddled with the latch sticking out of her laptop.

"Don't you think they should have already done those scientific tests?" she asked. "So when the first kids started asking questions—when *we* started asking questions—they could have presented us with evidence and proof and everything we needed to know? Since good old Dr. Grimaldi and Dr. Speck didn't see fit to tell us? Why *didn't* they just come out and tell us everything to begin with?"

Nick kept staring at his laptop screen, but Eryn could tell he wasn't reading anymore. His eyes had gone all unfocused and distant.

"What if they wanted it to be humans, not robots,

doing all those scientific tests?" Nick said. "Like, you know how Mom and Dad are always saying we have to do things for ourselves, instead of just having things handed to us. Like how I had to earn my own money for my new lacrosse stick, and Mom and Dad refused to pay for it?"

Eryn snorted.

"And you were lazy and took a whole year to earn enough?" she asked. "That was just about Mom and Dad trying to teach you a lesson. About responsibility, or whatever. This is about the fate of humanity. Why would anyone mess around with something so serious?"

Nick sat up straight, as if he had to defend his argument.

"I bet it is the same kind of thing," he said. "I bet humans themselves ruined humanity, and it's kind of like our generation has to earn back the right to live. I'm going to stop reading anything about volcanoes or other natural disasters."

"What if it's a natural disaster that humans caused?" Eryn asked. "Aren't we natural too?"

Nick didn't answer, because he was reading again. Eryn went back to reading too.

Contaminated water supplies . . . maybe. Naturally

occurring drought—I can skip that one, if Nick's right. A second Ice Age caused by human activity, out-of-control genetically modified food . . .

Beside her, Nick gasped.

"Did you see this?" he asked, holding out his laptop toward her.

Eryn leaned in.

Highlighted on the screen was a section beginning:

> I am a janitor at one of the banks where frozen human embryos continue to be kept. I don't know why humans went extinct, and unless I access others' memory banks, I know nothing of the science involved in theories about the extinction. But because of my position, I was one of the first individuals activated at the end of the Great Pause.

"The Great Pause?" Eryn repeated.

"That's what everyone keeps calling the time between the extinction and the birth of the first Snowflake," Nick said. "Haven't you noticed?"

Eryn didn't want to admit that she hadn't.

"Just checking," she said, and kept reading.

It was my job originally to make sure the embryo bank was clean and spotless and sterile before the arrival of the first embryos.

"Wait, if it's an embryo bank, weren't the embryos there all along?" Eryn asked.

"Keep going," Nick said.

Few realize that during the Great Pause the embryos were all stored in a top-secret location, not the current banks. So in those early days, before even the embryo scientists were awakened and activated, my embryo bank received shipment after shipment of automated frozen deliveries. One time I happened to see the GPS coordinates on one of the automated trucks making the delivery, showing where they were returning to for the next load. It was 37.1833 degrees north, 86.1000 degrees west.

I am just a janitor, and no one has ever issued an all-call before for information that I possess. Nobody but my fellow janitors have ever asked to access anything in my private memory banks. So I apologize if I seem presumptuous even bringing this up.

> But I have always thought that if there is any secret information hidden somewhere about the humans' last days—the previous humans' last days—then it would be in the same location where the embryos were originally kept during the Great Pause. So I felt duty-bound to mention this now. I apologize if I have inconvenienced anyone.

"He never even looked it up?" Eryn asked in amazement. "He never went there to check for himself?"

"Doesn't sound like it," Nick said, shrugging. "It's probably not in his programming to be curious."

"But where—" Eryn began.

Almost without thinking about it, she opened a search engine and started typing in the GPS coordinates the janitor had given. Nick was a step ahead of her—he was copying and pasting the numbers.

"It's in Kentucky?" he muttered. "But—it looks like those coordinates are in the middle of nowhere! There's nothing there!"

"Of course it'd say there's nothing there if it's some top-secret headquarters," Eryn said. She whirled around to face Mom's bedroom. "Mom! Mom! We've got to go to Kentucky! Now!"

FORTY

Eryn might have well have said, "Can we go next summer? Can we go sometime *before next winter?"* Nick thought despairingly.

As soon as Eryn asked, Mom promised to take them to check out the possibly secret location in Kentucky. But she said it would be about a six-hour trip, and it was already too late in the day to start traveling. The next day there was another bad storm forecast, and she said she didn't want to get caught in ice and snow. The next day she said Eryn seemed feverish and shouldn't be out and about.

"Of course I'm feverish!" Eryn had complained. "I'm in danger of going extinct!"

"Not helping," Nick whispered.

But they still had to wait another day.

Mom usually insisted they had to go to school unless they had one foot in the grave, but this week she made no mention of sending them back to school. She stayed home too, but seemed to have a lot she needed to do in her bedroom.

Eryn paced and ranted.

Nick kept going back to the computer research. He read everything anyone had sent in response to Mom's all-call, all the reasons humans might have all died out before, and might be doomed again. He asked Mom if they could go back to City Hall to watch the video of Dr. Grimaldi and Dr. Speck again. Mom sighed and said, "You don't actually have to go anywhere. . . ."

She picked up Nick's laptop, held it close to her body for a moment, and handed it back to him.

"Wireless transfer of selected sections of my memory," she said. "You'll see it in there labeled 'Grimaldi-Speck video.'"

Nick opened the file, and indeed, everything was there. At first he thought it was a slightly different video, filmed from a slightly different perspective. Then he realized it was just that this was from Mom's viewpoint, and she'd been sitting at a different angle to the screen than Nick had.

"This really is amazing," Nick muttered to himself.

"How can you stand watching that again and again

and again?" Eryn asked. "Don't you feel like giving up on Mom's promises and walking to Kentucky ourselves?"

"There might be clues in this we'll need once we get to Kentucky," Nick told her. "And—I'm looking for places the video might have been edited and spliced back together. Like if someone cut out the reason for the extinction."

"Oooh—I never thought of that!" Eryn said. She stopped her pacing and leaned over the back of the couch to look at the video herself. "Did you find any places where that happens?"

"Not that I can tell," Nick said. "It looks like they filmed this all in one take. So unless Dr. Speck and Dr. Grimaldi said what caused the extinction before they said hello or after they said good-bye, they never explained."

"Oh," Eryn said, slumping down against the back of the couch. Then she perked up again. "Unless they had such advanced technology back then that they could edit things to make it *look* like it was all one take. So we really don't know. Remember, they were ahead of things from the twenty-first century, since they took us 'back' to this time period."

"Yeah, that janitor even said there were automatic trucks at the end of the Great Pause," Nick agreed.

He wondered what those had been like. And what had happened to those trucks? Had they been melted down for scrap, like Michael said happened to the robot children who'd been twelve and younger? Or were they hidden somewhere? Was there maybe all sorts of advanced technology hidden in that secret headquarters in Kentucky?

"I wish *we* had automatic trucks, so we didn't need Mom to get us to Kentucky," Eryn moaned. "Tomorrow. If Mom doesn't get up first thing tomorrow morning ready to go to Kentucky, I really am going by myself. Even if there's a blizzard. Even if I'm sick as a dog. Are you in?"

Before Nick had a chance to answer, Mom came out of her bedroom.

"It's all arranged," she said. "Michael's picking up a rental van on his way home from work for us to use on our way to Kentucky. We'll leave first thing tomorrow morning."

"Finally!" Eryn exclaimed.

But Nick said, "Why do we need a rental van? Why don't we just use your car—or his?"

He was thinking about the soundproofing in Michael's car, about the way that would mean they wouldn't have to be careful about what they said.

FORTY-ONE

Eryn woke up in the middle of the night. Had she heard something? She tiptoed to her window, pushed aside the curtain, and looked out over the front yard. The eight-passenger van Michael had brought home was a hulking shadow in the driveway, a darker shape in the practically pitch-black night.

Something moved inside the van.

Eryn squinted. Was she imagining things? Was it just the reflection of a swaying branch in the van's windows or mirrors?

Her eyes adjusted. The darkness outside was not as complete as she'd thought. There was a little moonlight, and the snow still blanketing the ground gave off a dim glow, reflecting the moon's.

Someone *was* inside the van.

Michael.

As Eryn watched, her stepfather pressed his hands

Mom shook her head.

"Our cars don't have enough room," she said.

"What do you mean?" Eryn asked. "You, me, Nick, maybe an overnight bag for each of us—how much room does that take?"

"It's not just the three of us—everyone's going," Mom said.

"Everyone?" Nick repeated. He did not have a good feeling about this.

"Sure," Mom said. "The three of us. Michael. Dad. Brenda. And Ava and Jackson."

against the ceiling of the van, then against the frame above each door. He seemed to be pressing the upholstery into place, or perhaps sliding something underneath the upholstery.

Soundproofing, Eryn thought. *He's adding soundproofing to that van, so no one can overhear what anyone says while we're going to Kentucky.*

Eryn went back to bed and somehow managed to fall back to sleep.

In the morning everyone was in a rush, Mom nagging Nick and Eryn at every turn: "Hurry up and finish your breakfast before the others get here!" "Did you clean up your dishes?" "Did you remember to pack your toothbrush?"

Brenda, Ava, and Jackson arrived just as Eryn lugged her overnight bag down the stairs. The three of them stood awkwardly in the foyer. Ava and Jackson didn't even put down their bags.

"It must feel weird being here when Nick and I are here too," Eryn said, dropping her own bag to the floor when she reached the last step. "Like we've invaded your territory."

Ava flashed her sweetest smile, and it *seemed* genuine.

"Oh no, we don't mind at all," she said. "We don't think that way."

Yeah, no wonder Michael's worried that they don't seem like actual human kids, Eryn thought.

"Go ahead and take everything to the van," Mom said, carrying a bag of her own out of her bedroom. She turned and shouted up the stairs, "Nick! Come on!"

Dad arrived just as everyone was shoving bags into the back of the van.

"I'm here for the grand adventure!" he cried, springing out of his car. "Aren't we a great modern family? Spouses, ex-spouses, kids, and stepkids, all going on vacation together?"

He's not just saying that to remind Nick and me we're supposed to get along with Ava and Jackson, Eryn thought. It was more like he was announcing that to the whole world, trying to provide a cover story for their trip.

None of their neighbors were outside to hear him; in the still, frosty early-morning air, it was easy to believe that everyone in the neighborhood had decided to hibernate for the rest of the winter.

But obviously the grown-ups think somebody *could be listening;* somebody *could be suspicious and monitoring our conversation,* Eryn thought, stepping out of the way as Dad added his bag to the ones in the van and slammed the back door.

She flashed to her memory from the middle of the night of seeing Michael in the van, adding the soundproofing. That would make them safe from eavesdropping once they were in the van.

But what if that wasn't Michael I saw?

The thought seared through her.

It was so dark, and all I really saw was a shadowy figure—I just assumed it was Michael, she realized. *Because that's who I wanted it to be. What if it was someone completely different—an enemy? Someone might want to get rid of me and Nick because we know too much. And maybe someone knows about Ava and Jackson and would rather just get rid of them and Mom and Dad and Michael and Brenda in an "accident" rather than letting the rest of the world know how Michael broke the law. . . .*

What if Eryn had actually seen someone planting a bomb, not Michael trying to protect them?

She'd had three days of thinking about humans going extinct; three days of hearing Nick tell her all the theories of all the robots in the world about how humans could have destroyed themselves. All of those thoughts and theories *should* make her a lot more wary and suspicious.

"Eryn?" Mom said, and Eryn realized that the rest of her family—and Brenda, Ava, and Jackson—had already scrambled into the van and taken their seats. Eryn was the only one still standing in the driveway.

What if there was a bomb and it was set to go off as soon as everyone got in the van and shut the door? What if it was just set on a timer—and Mom and Michael had said a million times they were planning to leave promptly at eight a.m.?

Eryn glanced at her phone—it was three minutes until eight.

"Everyone but Michael get out!" Eryn screamed. "Now!"

All the robots—Mom, Dad, Michael, Brenda, Ava, and Jackson—instantly did exactly as Eryn said. Five of them scrambled out of the van; Michael stayed in the driver's seat. But Nick stayed huddled in his corner of the far backseat. He just glared at Eryn.

"What is wrong with you?" he asked. "You've been dying to get to Kentucky for three days! Just get in and let's go!"

Eryn didn't have time to argue with Nick. Not if it was already two minutes until eight. Every nerve in her body was screaming at her to run away from the van, but instead she dashed in and slammed the door.

"Michael!" she yelled, even as she climbed over the seats to get back to Nick, to pull him out if necessary. "Is it safe to say anything we want in this van? Was that you I saw in it in the middle of the night . . ."

Nick was still staring at her like she'd gone crazy, but Michael said in the calmest of voices, "That was me. And it *should* be safe, but let's not test it unless we have to. I had to do such a rush job. . . ."

Michael rolled down his window and leaned out.

"Okay everyone, we're fine," he told the others. "Come on back in. Just a moment of stepsibling panic. Nothing out of the ordinary. Donald, I guess you bragged too soon about how easily stepfamilies get along."

Eryn slumped down, her body sagging over the seats.

"What was *that* all about?" Nick muttered, still staring at her in dismay.

"I'll tell you later," Eryn muttered back. "When I'm sure it's safe."

But she'd seen how everyone but Nick had reacted so quickly when she'd screamed her command; she saw how cautiously they moved climbing back into the van.

It wasn't crazy to worry about bombs. It would be crazy not to worry about everything.

FORTY-TWO

They were barely out of Maywood when someone tapped Nick on the shoulder. It was Ava, turned around from the seat in front of him.

"Want to play cards?" she asked, holding up a deck. "Jackson and I know gin rummy, euchre, hearts, and of course all the little-kid games like go fish, old maid, and crazy eights. . . ."

"And poker," Jackson said, grinning in a way that seemed to imply he meant not just poker, but poker with gambling and actual money, which the adults would probably disapprove of.

"I don't really—" Nick began, but Ava leaned closer and whispered, "If we don't start something like this, bet you anything one of the grown-ups will insist we play the alphabet game. You know, where you have to find all the letters of the alphabet on billboards and license plates. You don't want to do that, do you?"

Nick didn't.

"All right," he said.

"Not me," Eryn said from the other side of the back bench seat. She didn't even turn her head, just kept her eyes trained on the snowdrifts speeding by.

"Euchre's out then, because we need four for that," Ava said. "And . . ."

She gestured toward the adults in the two rows at the front of the van, making it clear they were too far away to take part in a card game over the seats.

"How about hearts, then?" Nick asked, picking a game he barely knew. Dad had been on a kick for a while of trying to convince Nick that board games and card games were even more fun than video games, but it hadn't worked very well. Playing something called hearts just seemed the most . . . human. Humans had hearts. Robots didn't.

Stupid, he told himself a moment later as Ava dealt the cards with, well, robotic precision, using the seat back between them as a table. *Hearts is a game of strategy. You've got to be really good at keeping track of who picked up which cards. You're not going to outsmart robots at that!*

But it turned out that Jackson was a terrible hearts player. He lost every hand.

"What's your problem?" Ava finally asked him. "It's like you're trying to pick up the bad cards!"

"I am," Jackson said. "Ever heard of shooting the moon? If I get all the bad cards, I win and both of you lose! Everything flips around!"

Ava looked back and forth between Jackson and Nick. She put her cards down on her lap and pointed at Nick.

"Nick is also an adolescent boy," she said. "And *he* doesn't act like his brain is so soaked in testosterone that he can only do stupid, risky things! Don't you know you can only shoot the moon if you already have a really bad hand?"

"Maybe I'm just trying to psych you out," Jackson said, with a wicked grin. "Maybe I'm just tricking you into worrying that you have to pick up some of the bad cards yourself now, to stop me from getting them all!"

It was weird—after that, hearts started seeming like a really fun game. Nick had to watch both Ava and Jackson carefully, to see if they were trying to psych him out or not. He started ignoring the fact that they could be as stiff and formal and awkward as adults. He almost forgot that they weren't regular kids.

After a couple of hours they crossed the Ohio River;

an hour or so later they stopped for lunch at a Bob Evans that looked like it could have been the identical twin of the Bob Evans restaurant in Maywood. When they got back on the road, Michael switched to one of the passenger seats and Mom drove.

"Hey, Eryn, remember that time Mom took us to Niagara Falls right after Dad took us to the Crayola museum in Pennsylvania?" Nick asked. He guessed having divorced parents meant that they'd gotten about twice as many family vacations as most kids. "And you were upset because it was just water, not melted crayons, flowing over the falls?"

Eryn looked at him, rolled her eyes, and went back to staring out the window like she was a sentry who had to guard the whole family from danger. And she was just looking at a parking lot. A practically empty parking lot, because it was winter time, and no one would be out traveling now unless they had to.

"Oh, we went to Niagara Falls too," Ava said. "Did you do the Maid of the Mist tour and get totally soaked?"

Nick compared notes on family vacations with Ava and Jackson for a while. The grown-ups chimed in too. But Eryn never did.

By midafternoon they'd made it far enough south

that there were no more signs of snow. All the cities and towns seemed to have vanished too; hillsides full of nothing but leafless, dead-looking trees lined both sides of the highway.

Suddenly Mom swerved and pulled off the highway onto a small spit of gravel. Without discussing it, Dad, Michael, and Brenda hopped out of the van and began pulling branches out of the way so Mom could drive farther and farther into the woods. Maybe there had once been an actual road here, years ago; maybe that was why there was still gravel. But now it was amazing that Mom could keep going, angling the van between the trees, over a rise. By the time she came to a stop, she was far enough into the woods that probably nobody would be able to see them from the highway.

"Hey, my cell phone doesn't work here," Ava complained, holding up a jewel-studded iPhone.

"Neither does mine," Jackson added.

Nick started fumbling with his own pocket, but Eryn shook her head.

"Don't bother," she said. "It's time to stop pretending. This isn't a happy blended-family trip. We're here to hide."

Sure enough, one second later Mom commanded,

"Kids—all of you—hand over your cell phones."

Puzzled but obedient, Nick dug out his cell phone and passed it up to Mom. The other three kids did the same.

And then Mom put all four of the phones on the floor of the van, pulled out a hammer, and swung it down on the pile of phones.

FORTY-THREE

I really am a twenty-first-century kid, Eryn thought. *Even after everything else that's happened, that was one of the scariest things I've ever witnessed: seeing my mother destroy my cell phone.*

Even after six hours of staring out a car window imagining horrors at every turn, she'd still been tempted to scream, watching Mom swing the hammer at the phones.

This is real, Eryn thought. *We really are in danger. Mom doesn't believe in destroying* anything. *She believes in reduce, reuse, recycle—not pounding perfectly good phones down to nothingness.*

Ava and Jackson watched open-mouthed. Nick started to protest, but Eryn shook her head at him.

"Phones have tracking, remember?" she said.

Nick gazed wide-eyed back and forth between Mom and Eryn.

"But then—couldn't anyone have tracked us here already? *Are* we where we need to be?" he asked.

Michael was sliding open the door of the van. He didn't look surprised by the pile of smashed cell phone parts on the floor next to Mom.

So he knew she was going to do that, Eryn thought. *They planned it all ahead. . . .*

"We're going the rest of the way on foot," Michael said. "It'd be smart to carry only what you absolutely have to have in these backpacks."

He started handing out small black backpacks. Eryn unzipped hers and saw that it already contained a water bottle and some energy bars and trail mix. There wasn't room for much more than a change of clothes.

They planned this out too, Eryn thought.

Nick was still gazing at the pile of phone parts.

"But—we have very precise GPS coordinates to follow," he said. "We need GPS! If one of you grown-ups was counting on using some GPS thingy in your head, won't that send out our location too?"

"We're going old-school," Michael said, holding up a small, flat wooden box and a folded paper. "Compass and map."

That silenced Nick. Eryn noticed that Brenda was

slowly walking around the van, holding her hands out in front of her.

"This does seem to be a complete dead zone," she said. "I'm not sensing any signals, in or out."

Isn't that what you would expect for a top-secret headquarters? Eryn wondered, her heart beating faster.

"This way," Michael said, heading deeper into the woods, farther from the highway.

Silently everyone loaded their backpacks, strapped them on, and then fell into line behind him. The trees were so close together that there was only room to go single file. Mom and Michael were in the lead, then all the kids, then Dad and finally Brenda.

Are the adults trying to protect us by being in the front and the back, in case anyone attacks? Eryn wondered.

But who would attack them? And they'd already been in remote areas the past few hours—if anyone was going to attack, wouldn't it have already happened?

It's more likely that the adults are making sure none of us kids runs ahead or straggles behind and gets lost, Eryn thought.

They trampled on. Leafless, dead-seeming branches and twigs constantly snagged at their clothes and had to be pulled away; old, dead fallen leaves slipped and slid beneath their feet, making the path treacherous.

But Eryn was starting to think that maybe they were on an actual trail, or at least the ghost of one. Maybe a long time ago this had been a paved road or a bike path. Under the layers of dead leaves, Eryn caught sight of gravel and what might have been bits of broken-up asphalt.

The gap between the trees widened a bit, and Eryn sped up and walked beside Nick. Everyone else walked alongside someone now too: Mom with Michael, Ava with Jackson, and at the back, Brenda and Dad.

"Two by two," Nick muttered. "Remember that story Mom used to read us when we were little? About the guy who saved a pair of every kind of animal? Noah's Boat, or something like that?"

"Ark," Eryn said. "It was Noah's Ark. That's the kind of boat he built. That story always confused me so much. I never understood how that Noah guy knew to save the animals, when no one else even knew to save themselves."

"Maybe it was one of those stories missing something from religion or philosophy," Nick said. "Something robots can't understand, so we don't understand it either."

"Maybe," Eryn said.

She hadn't thought of the Noah's Ark story in years, but remembering it now just scared her more. What were she and Nick missing? What if there was something really, really essential they needed to know—that they didn't know because they'd been raised by robots?

Michael and Mom stopped at the front of the line. Michael kept looking back and forth between the compass and the map.

"It's hard to be totally accurate without GPS, but I think we're generally in the right vicinity for those coordinates you kids found," he said. "Maybe if we all just look around a little?"

Eryn's heart sank. They were surrounded by trees with dead-looking leafless branches soaring overhead, and thick layers of decaying dead leaves underfoot. That's what they'd been surrounded by for the past hour. What if the janitor at the embryo bank had been totally wrong about the coordinates he'd seen on the automatic truck? What if he'd been right, and even though there'd been an embryo bank here twelve or thirteen years ago, there was nothing here now?

What if Eryn and Nick had no other clue to go on?

We don't have any other clue to go on, she told herself.

She shuffled off the path slightly, but her heart wasn't in it.

"Don't go far," Mom warned. "Remember, if anyone gets lost, we don't have any way to find you electronically."

Somehow that worked on Eryn like reverse psychology, and she took a big step outward; she leaned even farther over a huge fallen tree.

"What's that?" she asked, pointing downhill through gnarled branches. She could just barely see something like a huge humped arch of stone.

Nick craned his neck behind her.

"Is it a cave?" he asked. His face lit up. "It *is* a cave! Wouldn't a cave be a great place to have a secret headquarters?"

And then he took off running.

FORTY-FOUR

Nick didn't even have to glance back over his shoulder to know that Eryn was right behind him. He knew he could count on her running too.

Right now he didn't care if the others came with them or not. He needed *answers.* And they were so close now, he'd do anything he could to get them as fast as possible.

It was messy running downhill, his shoes skidding and slipping on the wet leaves. More than once he had to touch his fingertips down into the mud to keep his balance; more than once he scrapped his shins against fallen logs or upended tree trunks. But he kept going.

The cave ahead of them was *huge.* Just the mouth of it was probably as tall as a two- or three-story building. A small waterfall trickled down from the top, and the individual falling droplets made Nick think of some giant beast's teeth.

"Stop!" Mom shouted behind them, and Nick felt her grab his arm, jerking him backward. She did the same to Eryn, and Mom's pull was so strong that all three of them landed on their rears in the cold half-frozen mud.

"But, Mom, I'm sure that's got to be where the embryos were," Eryn protested. "I'm sure that's where the answers are."

"Don't you see the signs?" Mom said.

Nick looked again.

Now he noticed that there were heavy chains linked across the opening of the cave, down near the bottom. He had to squint to see letters on rusty metal placards hanging from the chains and plastered against the hill-side. The signs had obviously been there a long time; they blended into the rock. Many of them were covered by old, dead ivy vines.

"Geez, Mom, even if you're just supposed to have normal robot vision, it must still be better than ours," Nick muttered.

"Those say, 'Keep Out! Mammoth Cave is susceptible to cave-ins and sinkholes! Danger!'" Mom said.

Nick yanked his arm away from Mom and leaned forward. Now he could also make out the words *Danger!* and *Keep Out!* in the ancient rusty letters.

"You are *not* going in there," Mom lectured them. "If it wasn't safe whenever those signs were made, it certainly isn't safe now. Besides, if someone knew the secret to saving an entire species, who would hide it in such a dangerous place?"

Mom turned back to the others, to wave them away from the danger. So only Nick heard what Eryn whispered:

"Humans would do that. To keep the secret."

FORTY-FIVE

We have to get into that cave when nobody's watching.

The words buzzed in Eryn's head so loudly she was afraid everyone could hear them; surely everyone could tell what she was thinking just by looking at her. But somehow only Nick seemed to understand. Their eyes met and he nodded.

"Come on away from there," Dad shouted from above them on the hill.

Reluctantly, Eryn turned back.

Later, she told herself. *We'll find a way.*

It was a lot harder scrambling back up the hillside than it had been slipping and sliding and running down. By the time she and Nick reached the top again, everyone was turned toward Ava and Jackson.

"Look what we found!" Ava called.

She was trying to lift a large sign that seemed to have toppled from a rock base. This sign was made of some sort of plastic or laminate, so it wasn't as weathered and hard to read as the metal ones.

Ava and Jackson got the sign up at an angle. Now Eryn could see that it said "Mammoth Cave National Park" in large letters and then, in smaller letters below, "A World Heritage Site and International Biosphere Reserve."

"This isn't a national park!" Nick exclaimed. "We'd know about it! Remember I did that national parks project in school last year? None of them are in Kentucky! None of them are called Mammoth Cave!"

"Maybe this used to be a national park," Mom said. "Before. But then with the sinkholes and all, it wouldn't be safe for tourists to come here now."

"I wonder how many other things have changed from before," Jackson said.

Eryn glanced at him with new respect. That was something she'd been wondering herself, ever since she'd seen the video of Dr. Grimaldi and Dr. Speck. She remembered how Dr. Speck had put it: "Of course, we're still very human. We couldn't resist some tinkering. When we saw the opportunity to make improvements, we did try that."

Dr. Grimaldi, Dr. Speck, and the others who worked

with them had changed more than just the things that might lead to another extinction.

But shutting down an entire national park? Eryn thought. *That seems suspicious.*

Wasn't that proof—or almost proof—that this was meant to be a top-secret place, a place where secrets were hidden?

Eryn worked to keep her face smooth, hiding her suspicions.

Nick sat down on the pile of tumbled-down rocks that had probably once held the Mammoth Cave sign.

"I'm so tired," he said. He looked beseechingly at the grown-ups. "Please tell me the reason your backpacks are bigger than ours is that you've got tents and sleeping bags and stuff like that for camping out here overnight. It's going to be dark soon. I don't think I could hike all the way back to the van right now."

Okay, not a bad strategy, Nick, Eryn thought. *We have to convince the grown-ups we have to stay here longer, and overnight is a great idea. But are you maybe being a little too obvious?*

Maybe not. Michael gave the ghost of a grin, and started unzipping his backpack. He started pulling out pieces that clicked together and made . . .

An ax? Eryn wondered.

"We don't exactly have tents and sleeping bags," Michael said. "But we're going to test our mountaineering skills. We can stay in the woods tonight, but it will be more pioneer style. Roughing it. I think we have just enough light left for putting together a rough lean-to. Who wants to help?"

No one answered that question. Ava's eyes grew wide.

"But . . . but . . . I thought we'd be in a hotel," she said. She turned toward Brenda. "You said this would be like an ordinary family vacation, just with more people."

Eryn had had it with that "family vacation" pretense.

"I think what your parents—and mine—didn't tell us was that they mostly want to lay low for a while," she said. She narrowed her eyes at Michael. "Right? Because of the attention on Nick and me, you're more afraid than ever that someone's going to find out the truth about Ava and Jackson. Aren't you?"

"Well, um . . . ," Michael said, darting his eyes toward Ava and Jackson.

"Dad?" Ava said, her voice high and panicky. "Mom?"

Brenda put her arm around Ava's shoulder.

"This will just be a wonderful adventure out in

nature," Brenda said soothingly. "Surrounded by people you love. And by people who love you."

You don't go camp out in the woods in the middle of winter to have a wonderful adventure in nature, Eryn thought. *You only do that in the spring, summer, or fall.*

She'd just been throwing out a random accusation, but everything made sense. Keeping Ava and Jackson out in the woods also kept them away from electronic surveillance, from the danger that anyone else would find out that they weren't human children.

Good grief, Eryn thought. *How long do the grown-ups plan to keep Ava and Jackson here? How long do they plan to keep* us *here?*

Michael stepped toward Eryn.

"Please don't say anything else to set my kids off," he said under his breath. "They're at a very fragile stage of their development, both of them."

And Nick and I aren't? Eryn wanted to spit back at him. *Aren't we fragile because of the big revelation we heard just a couple of days ago? Aren't we're in danger of going extinct? The fact that everyone like us could die—doesn't that* prove *we're fragile?*

She bit her tongue. It would be easier to sneak out

later and go back to the cave if she acted like she was going along with things now.

"Hey, Ava, let's go look for dry wood we can use for kindling," Eryn called. "I'm sure you'll feel a lot better once we're sitting around a roaring fire. And I don't know about your dad, but I bet my dad brought marshmallows for us to roast!"

Dad grinned and began unzipping his backpack. Eryn wasn't sure if he really had brought marshmallows, or if he was just teasing them with the possibility. Mom nodded approvingly. Jackson picked up a handful of sticks.

Eryn couldn't believe that the others seemed to be falling for her suggestion.

Either that, or they were as desperate to keep up a pretense as she was.

FORTY-SIX

The grown-ups aren't worried about smoke giving away our location, Nick thought, lying on the ground later that night and staring into the fire that all four of the kids had helped build. *They're not worried about anything but electronic tracking.*

Of course, that was because they were robots, and they were only worried about other robots finding them. As far as Nick knew, smoke could only be detected by others nearby, and obviously the eight of them were miles away from the nearest living soul. Or the nearest functioning robot.

Nick snuggled deeper beneath the "blanket" Mom had tucked him under for the night—which was mostly just leaves piled on top of his coat and jeans. A log collapsed in the fire, sending off a burst of sparks, which quickly faded into the darkness. On the other side of the fire, Ava and Jackson didn't even jump.

Have they finally fallen asleep? Nick wondered.

"It's a shame we don't have pillows and blankets to make it look like we're tucked in and sleeping soundly like good little kids, even when we aren't," Eryn whispered beside him.

"We could leave our coats behind, wrapped around logs," Nick whispered back.

Even he wasn't sure this was a good idea—it was pretty cold outside—but he could tell that Eryn was shrugging her coat off next to him. If she was willing to risk the cold, how could he chicken out?

Nick cast a quick glance at the lumps arrayed around the fire a little farther out than Ava and Jackson: Mom, Michael, Dad, and Brenda. Dad seemed to be snoring, and his messy hair cast odd shadows blowing about in the slight breeze.

None of the other adults moved. Were they all asleep?

"We'll go quietly, one at a time, and wait by that tree over there," Eryn whispered, pointing downhill into darkness. "If anyone notices us leaving, we can just say we have to pee."

Nick nodded, feeling grateful that Eryn had everything figured out. Silently he eased off his coat, slid it to the ground, and piled leaves on top of it. That was good enough. The coat alone would look like a sleeping body, as long as nobody looked too closely. But now he had on only a flannel shirt and jeans, and he couldn't resist rubbing his arms.

"It'll be warmer in the cave," Eryn whispered. "Aren't caves a constant temperature year-round?"

She tiptoed past him. When she reached the tree she'd pointed at before, she gave a quick glance around and then signaled for Nick to follow.

Nick looked once more at everyone sleeping by the fire. Nobody had moved. He decided it was safe to tiptoe toward Eryn.

"We're going to need some kind of light," he whispered. "I could barely see you signaling. Should we take a branch from out of the fire? Like, make it into some kind of torch?"

"I already swiped Michael's flashlight when he wasn't looking," Eryn said, holding out the pocket of her sweatshirt. That must be where she'd stashed it.

"Sweet!" Nick said. "But—did you get back-up batteries? What if it dies when we're halfway into the cave and we can't get back out?"

Something about going into a dangerous place to find

out what had once killed off his entire species made him unusually cautious. Almost panicky, though he didn't want Eryn to see that.

"This is *Michael's* flashlight we're talking about," Eryn said. "It's high-tech, with every bell and whistle. And a battery-life gauge. It looks like it's got thirty hours left. We'll be fine. But I want to wait until we're away from camp before I turn it on."

The two of them started easing down the hillside they'd run down before. It was harder than ever in the dark, and Nick kept tripping. He looked back, and they were far enough away now that he could no longer see the fire, only smoke.

"It'd be better for you to turn that flashlight on now, than for us to wake up everyone screaming when we fall to the bottom of the hill," he told Eryn.

He expected her to argue just on principle, but she pulled the flashlight out of her pocket and switched it on. The weak glow seemed to make barely a dent in the darkness around them. Having a little light was almost scarier, because it cast such shadows.

Eryn linked her elbow through Nick's.

"This way, if one of us starts to fall, the other one can catch him," she whispered.

Nick could have said, *Catch "him"? You think I'd be the one to fall?* He could have said, *Wait—doesn't this make it more likely that if one of us starts to fall, both of us do?*

But he kind of liked holding on to Eryn, and having her hold on to him.

He didn't say anything, just held on tighter.

Slowly, gradually, slipping and sliding, they made their way down the hill. When they reached the bottom, the cave opening seemed even more enormous than before. Eryn shone her flashlight into the heart of it, but the paltry beam was just swallowed up; the cave seemed like nothing but a pit of darkness.

Eryn giggled.

"If they really wanted to keep people out, don't you think they should have used something more than chains?" she asked. She let go of Nick to step over the rusty links. "A barbed-wire fence, maybe? An *electrified* fence?"

Nick held his breath, but nothing happened to Eryn. A sinkhole didn't open up in the ground to swallow her up. The ceiling of the cave didn't fall on her head.

He stepped over the chains as well.

"I guess they thought the signs would do the trick,"

Nick said. "They thought people would obey the signs."

He slid his feet tentatively forward. The ground under his feet felt perfectly solid and safe.

Eryn snorted.

"They thought *robots* would obey the signs," she said. "Robots follow rules. That's what they're programmed to do."

Nick put his hand on Eryn's arm.

"Eryn—how many times have you ever seen a grown-up break a rule?" he asked. "Except for Michael and Brenda making Ava and Jackson, have you ever seen a grown-up do anything wrong?"

He racked his brain, trying to think of even the most minor infraction. Dropping a wad of gum on the school floor? Switching cafeteria trays to get someone else's larger serving of chocolate pudding? Shoving a friend's books off his desk because you were mad? He'd seen lots of kids do stuff like that, but never a grown-up.

"Dad yelled at us that one time," Eryn said. "When we were asking him questions about Ava and Jackson."

"He barely raised his voice," Nick scoffed. "And . . . it was connected to Ava and Jackson. Those are the only things we can think of."

He put aside everything he wondered about Ava and

Jackson, because something else intrigued him more right now.

"I always thought grown-ups didn't break rules just because they were grown-ups," he said. "And . . . that we'd be like that too, in another ten or twenty years. But we won't, will we? Geez, what do you think the world's going to be like once it's all humans in charge again?"

Eryn took the thought in a completely different direction.

"What do you bet those signs were just there to keep out the robots, then?" she asked. "I bet this cave is perfectly safe, it's just that there are *tons* of secrets here. Not just about the extinction, but—everything! Everything we humans need to find out for ourselves!"

"But—" Nick started to object. It seemed like there might be lots of dangers connected to what they'd both just figured out.

It was too late. Eryn was already rushing ahead of him, deeper into the cave.

FORTY-SEVEN

Everything about the cave terrified Eryn. It was so dark—her flashlight beam seemed practically useless against the thick blackness pressing in on her and Nick. And with so little ability to see, she found that even the tiniest sound was magnified and turned horrific. Water dripped ominously somewhere farther in, again and again and again.

Then she heard a sound like a pebble falling.

Is that going to turn into an avalanche of falling rock? Eryn wondered. *Right on top of us? Were we total idiots for ignoring the "keep out" signs, and now we're going to die for our own stupidity?*

Mom and Dad would be so sad. Even if they were robots.

Eryn froze, but the sound stopped. And then she forced herself to go on. Each step reminded her exactly how much she was a child of civilization. She wanted bright glowing electric lights that banished any hint of shadow from every corner of the cave. For that matter, she didn't even want to *be* in a cave—she'd rather be looking for answers in clean, tidy rooms with no strange sounds that might be bats or mice or the beginnings of a rockslide.

But she kept going. She did her best not to let Nick see how scared she was.

Then something struck her that she couldn't help sharing.

"Remember back at the beginning, when we first heard about Ava and Jackson?" she asked Nick, even as they inched deeper and deeper into the darkness. "Didn't you think, *Oh, if I just find out what sports they play, or whether they like art or music—then I'll know what they're like?*"

"I guess," Nick said.

"That's not even true about us," Eryn said. "Maybe it is for some kids, but . . . I don't care that much about tennis or being in the school play. I don't even think you care that much about lacrosse. *This* is what we're like. This is our true identities. That we nagged Mom to bring us down here. That we're walking into a supposedly dangerous cave because we *have* to get answers."

"Is that just what we're like, or is that what all humans are like?" Nick asked quietly.

"I don't know," Eryn admitted.

They kept creeping forward. Every few steps, Eryn would sweep the flashlight all around, in case there was something important off to the side or overhead they might have missed otherwise.

There never was. Rock, rock, dripping rock, shadowy rock . . .

Eryn took a few more steps, stopped, and did another sweep with the flashlight.

"What's that?" Nick gasped.

Eryn moved her flashlight ever so slightly backward and squinted into the shadows.

"I don't see anything," she said.

"Isn't that a doorknob?" Nick asked, pointing.

Eryn was about to say, *It's just another rock. Rock formations look like doorknobs all the time. Especially in caves.* But just to be sure, she took a step toward the wall Nick was pointing at. She held the flashlight steadier.

It *was* a doorknob they were both staring at. Surrounded by a door built solidly into a doorframe in the rock wall.

"Who would put a door in a cave?" Eryn asked, rushing forward. "It doesn't make sense."

"Humans don't make sense," Nick whispered. He was right on her heels.

They had to climb over a small pile of rock rubble on the floor, which made Eryn think uncomfortably of rock falls, but they kept going.

"If it's locked, we'll figure out how to pick it," Nick said. "We've got experience."

Eryn moaned.

"I don't have any bobby pins with me," she said. "I didn't think—"

"We'll find a really sturdy twig," Nick said. "Or we'll figure out how to rig up the batteries from the flashlight into some kind of explosive and blow the door open."

"You're crazy!" Eryn said, half laughing and half convinced she'd be right there with him building bombs, if need be.

But she reached for the doorknob, and none of that mattered.

The doorknob turned easily as soon as she grasped it. The door swung open.

FORTY-EIGHT

"Shine the light in—let me see!" Nick called, grabbing for the flashlight in Eryn's hand so he could direct its beam too.

The light beam spun crazily, out of control. With both of them trying to move it, it zoomed over everything too quickly for Nick to figure out what he was seeing. But Eryn gasped, "Oooo, there's a light switch!"

Nick started to complain, *That's not going to work. Not after centuries.* But Eryn had already reached over to the wall beside them and flipped the switch.

Light poured down on them from above. After all the darkness, this was like being doused in light, being drenched with it.

It was so bright, Nick couldn't see.

He blinked frantically, his eyes finally managing to focus on the center of the door they'd just opened.

There was another "Keep out!" sign on it. Before, he'd been too intent on the doorknob to notice.

"Oh, right, because they didn't *already* tell us to keep out," Nick muttered.

"No, Nick, *look*," Eryn said.

Her hand shook as she pointed at small print at the bottom of the sign: "Absolutely no robots allowed past this point. No robots allowed into this room."

"We were right," Eryn whispered. "They did want humans to be the first to find this secret."

Because . . . it's so much fun finding out for ourselves how people can all die? Nick thought uncomfortably.

"Finally we can find out how to save humanity," Eryn said, almost as if she knew what Nick was thinking, and she wanted to flip his ideas around.

Nick blinked again—just like Mom—and turned away from the door, toward the open room before him. It had a black-and-white tile floor that reminded him of the cafeteria at school. The walls were a pleasant light gray. And the only furniture was a glass-topped desk right in the center of the room.

"Their technology had to have been more advanced than ours," Eryn said in a hushed voice. Nick wasn't sure if she was whispering because she was awestruck or because she was scared. "Remember, they had already gotten past the early twenty-first century. That's why they have lights that will still turn on after hundreds of years. And this room must have been airtight. Look how there aren't any spiderwebs or dust or mouse droppings. . . ."

Nick stepped forward, and he knew he was leaving footprints, since his shoes were dirty from walking through the cave. He shoved the door shut behind him so at least they wouldn't let anything worse in.

He was mostly just relieved that they hadn't found skeletons.

"Okay, so to find out all the secrets, we're probably going to have to figure out how to operate something that's, like, the great-great-grandson of an iPad," Nick said. "Whatever we're looking for, I bet it's in that desk."

Together the two of them walked to the desk. But there wasn't any sign of anything like an iPad. The glass on the top of the desk was smoky and impossible to see through. And though they both tried to get a grip on the glass to lift it, it seemed to be locked down tight.

"Maybe the desk itself is the computer?" Eryn suggested. "Like maybe computers got big again, instead of always getting smaller? Where do you think we turn it on?"

She began feeling along the sides of the desk.

"Doesn't this kind of remind you of something?" Nick asked. "Like . . . remember when Mom took us to Washington, D.C., and showed us the Constitution and the Declaration of Independence at the National Archives?"

"You think this is the same kind of display case?" Eryn asked. "What'd the guide call the ones there—'hermetically sealed'?"

Nick began running his fingers underneath the display case. He heard a click—and the glass lid of the case slowly began to rise.

"Oh, good job!" Eryn said, crouching down to see whatever was in the desk that much sooner, before the glass lid opened all the way.

Nick did the same.

Inside was a stack of papers.

"They didn't get more technologically advanced—they went old-school," Nick whispered.

Then he saw what was handwritten on the top of the stack: "For human eyes only. Absolutely no robots are allowed to read these papers."

"Okay, okay, we get the message," Nick muttered. "This is something we've got to do for ourselves. Our mommies and daddies aren't allowed to baby us anymore."

Eryn reached out and pulled aside the top sheet of paper. Underneath was another handwritten page that began, "Instructions for the new generation of humanity . . ."

Eryn had always been a little faster at reading than Nick was. So he heard her gasp. And then he saw why.

The rest of the hand-scrawled message on the second sheet of paper was:

"Our own robots were the ones who destroyed us. You must destroy your robots before they destroy you."

FORTY-NINE

Eryn took a shaky step back.

"Our robots? Mom and Dad?" she whispered. "They mean we have to destroy our own parents? *Kill* them?"

"There's got to be some mistake," Nick muttered. "Or this is a joke. A *bad* joke."

The glass lid, which had continued rising, began wobbling back and forth, as if it were meant to go still higher but had gotten stuck.

And then it broke off its hinges and crashed to the floor in an explosion of glass.

Eryn and Nick both jumped back, but Eryn guessed that they still ended up with tiny shards of glass on their clothes.

They were both too stunned even to brush themselves off.

At least we're not hurt, Eryn thought. *At least the ceiling didn't cave in on us; at least the ground didn't fall out from under our feet.*

Wasn't being told that they needed to destroy their own parents worse than any of those things?

"See, even their mechanized desks don't work right," Nick said. He probably meant it to be funny, but his voice trembled too much. It just made Eryn want to cry.

"Nothing works perfectly every single time," Eryn said, and her voice came out sounding like a whimper.

"Probably the robots who destroyed the humans, they probably just . . . ," Nick began.

Eryn knew what he was thinking. There could have been some problem, one that turned robots into killers the humans couldn't stop.

"But the robots we have now, the ones like Mom and Dad—they wouldn't kill anyone," Eryn said. "They're working the way they're supposed to."

"Except that Michael and Brenda created Ava and Jackson," Nick said numbly. "They went against their programming for *that.*"

Eryn found herself clutching the side of the desk. She had to, to hold herself up. Her ears were ringing, and she wasn't sure if it was because of the crashing glass or just shock.

Did you think there was going to be something cheerful about finding out what made humans go extinct? she wondered.

She hadn't. But she had kind of expected joy—and maybe even fame and glory—in finding out how to stop humans from going extinct again.

She hadn't expected to be told she needed to kill her parents, and everyone else's, too.

How would anyone even do that?

She pushed the thought away. She wasn't considering doing what the writing on the paper told her to do. It could just be the scrawling of a madman. It could be utterly meaningless.

She already knew it was vile and cruel—and inhuman.

"Maybe we should at least read what else it says in these papers?" Nick suggested in a small voice.

Eryn didn't trust her own voice to respond, but she nodded.

"We can split it in half so we get through it faster," Nick said, reaching for the papers.

Eryn blindly took the half of the stack he handed her. Both of them sank to the floor and began reading.

Evidently hers was the bottom half, because her first page started in the middle of a sentence: ". . . were on a quest to build superintelligent computers, artificial intelligence that would far surpass our own limited human capabilities . . ."

Somehow Eryn seemed to have lost the ability to read words in order, one after another, all the way down a page. Every time she tried, her eyes jumped ahead or began to see other words superimposed atop the actual words on the paper.

The words she kept seeing were: "You must destroy your robots. . . . You must destroy your robots. . . ."

She found the best she could do was just skip around, grasping a phrase or two at a time: "military implications . . . sending robotic creatures into war zones rather than risking soldiers' lives . . . became efficient killing machines, unsurpassed in their ability to extinguish human life . . . began to think for themselves, completely outside our control . . ."

In spite of herself, her mind started putting together a story, figuring out a connection between the phrases.

The military had been trying to save lives—human lives. They'd come up with robots to send into battle so human soldiers didn't have to die.

The robots were really good at killing. That's what they were *for*.

But then the humans lost control of the robots. They couldn't be stopped.

The robots began killing everyone.

I guess they weren't programmed to count embryos

in embryo banks as human, Eryn thought. *So they didn't kill us, too.*

People like Dr. Grimaldi and Dr. Speck had known that. They must not have known how to stop the killing robots, but they knew how to start humanity again, after all the killing was over.

They just had to rely on robots, the same type of creatures that had killed all of humanity in the first place.

And then, once the human race was established again, they wanted Eryn and Nick and the rest of their generation to destroy their robots before humanity was destroyed once again.

"But the robots now—Mom and Dad—they weren't designed to kill us," Eryn moaned. "It's different."

Her eyes fell on a line on the papers that might as well have been an answer to her moan: ". . . clear that robots will always evolve, just like living things . . . it's inevitable that humans lose control of what their creations become . . ."

Just like Michael and Brenda had defied their programming to create Ava and Jackson.

"Ready to trade?" Nick asked beside her.

Silently Eryn handed him the papers she'd been reading, and took his stack instead. But she didn't bend her head to look down at the pages.

"Do you hear something?" she asked. "Outside?"

Distantly, even with the door shut, she could still hear the dripping of water somewhere out there in the enormous space known as Mammoth Cave. It'd been there the whole time, a background noise she'd tuned out while they'd turned on the light, discovered the desk, shattered the glass, and read the horrifying papers.

But something about the dripping sound had changed. That was what made her notice it again. It wasn't just dripping. Was it maybe also the sound of . . .

Footsteps?

Eryn clutched Nick's arm.

"Listen!" she hissed, leaning close. "What if some of those killer robots are hiding in the back of the cave? What if they heard us come in here? What if—"

Nick looked up. His eyes looked so big and terrified they seemed to take up his whole face. Eryn guessed he'd put together as much of the story of the extinction as she had.

"The signs on the door," he said. "And at the front of the cave. They'd keep robots out. All robots."

There were definitely footsteps sounding outside the door. They were definitely coming toward this room.

Then the door began to open.

FIFTY

Nick stuffed the papers he was holding into his shirt. Eryn started to shove hers into her sweatshirt pocket, but they didn't fit. She thrust them at Nick instead. This told him they both still had hope. Hope that they could keep these papers secret. Hope that whoever they were about to face could still be reasoned with, maybe even fooled into thinking that Nick and Eryn were too sweet and innocent and ignorant to be killed.

Oh no, Mr. Killer Robot, I don't know that you're a killer. I just think of robots as . . . part of the family.

But the papers in his hands and the ones jabbing his stomach said even the robots in his own family could be killers. Even the robots in his own family should be killed.

Nick jammed Eryn's papers into his shirt too. The door kept opening. It was open far enough now that Nick could see . . .

Mom. And Dad, Michael, Brenda, Ava, and Jackson.

Nick felt everything at once: relief and fear, fear and relief. . . . His heart raced and slowed and raced again.

What were he and Eryn supposed to do now?

"There you are!" Mom cried, rushing toward him and Eryn. "We were so worried!"

She knelt before them, wrapping her arms around both of them, drawing them close, mashing them into a huge hug.

Nick was too overcome to do anything but let himself be hugged. He flopped against Eryn as if the two of them were nothing but rag dolls.

But the papers . . . what if the papers fall out and Mom sees them? he wondered.

The folded pages stabbed against his bare skin, but Mom had on her winter coat and a fleece underneath that. Surely she couldn't feel them.

Still, the rustle of the papers beneath his shirt woke up Nick's brain. He had to cover for the noise.

"But—those signs," Nick mumbled into Mom's hair as she continued hugging him. "'Absolutely no robots allowed.' How could you go past those signs? Wasn't that against your programming?"

Mom made a sound that could have been an amused snort or the beginning of sobs. It reminded Nick of hearing Jackson break down.

"You're forgetting the parental imperative," she said. She kept her head between Nick's and Eryn's, and pressed them close.

Nick pulled back. Eryn did too.

"The parental what?" Eryn asked.

Back at the door, Michael chuckled.

"I'll translate," he said. "She means we're programmed to be parents first and foremost. If there's a contradiction in orders or programming, our parental instincts win. So parents *have* to go after children in danger, even at risk to their own lives."

Nick glanced at Eryn, wanting to tell her, *See? That means our parents could never kill us! We're fine!*

Eryn squinted back at him, and he wondered if she was thinking the same thing that popped into his own head next: *Yes, but somebody else's parents wouldn't mind killing us. We're not every robot's kids.*

Eryn's squint intensified.

"Ava and Jackson aren't anyone's parents," she said. "*They* don't have children in danger. So how'd they manage to disobey the signs?"

"Oh, I didn't program them to think of themselves as robots," Michael said.

Nick didn't even have to look at his sister again to know that she would be staring pointedly at him, thinking with laser intensity, *See? See? They're the ones we have to worry about!*

"Even if we aren't your parents, we wanted to make sure you were safe," Ava said softly, tilting her heart-shaped face.

She looked more like a kitten than a killer. She sounded so sincere.

"We woke up and heard the grown-ups talking," Jackson said. "So we followed our dad and your parents into the cave. We wanted to rescue you too! And Mom followed us. Because, duh, then she thought *her* kids were in danger."

"And all of you kids are in so much trouble," Dad said, shaking his head so hard his hair flaired out. Mom was usually much more into discipline than he was, so having him scold them made it seem worse. "Putting yourselves in danger—for what?"

"We had to . . . ," Eryn began. She glanced at Nick and let her voice trail off.

Mom sighed and settled back into a crouch before them. She kept her hands on their shoulders.

"Eryn, Nick, I know this past week has been hard on you," she said. "I know everything you found out has been a jolt, and you've gotten this strange obsession with finding answers to *all* your questions. But I've studied human psychology—centuries worth of it—and it is the nature of human life that there is always something that's a mystery. That's a fact we just couldn't explain to you when you were younger. But you're old enough to understand that now. It's part of the transition to adulthood. Accepting that you're never going to have all your questions answered."

She glanced around, her sharp eyes seeming to take in every corner of the room.

Look what you found," she said. "An empty room and a broken desk. That's all. That's all you'll ever find, looking for the past. Because if there was more you were supposed to know about the extinction, we'd already know it."

She really didn't feel the papers through her coat, Nick thought. This time, he was very careful not to glance at Eryn. It seemed like even a tiny turn of the head would give away that the two of them were keeping secrets. But he could practically feel Eryn thinking along with him: *None of the grown-ups—none of the robots—know about the papers. They won't know anything unless we tell them. And we're not going to.*

Mom was still talking, still in her calm, soothing

school-psychologist voice. "I let you look at my generation's ideas for what might have caused the extinction because I thought you would see a natural conclusion: With the changes the previous humans made—their arrangements for the reawakening of human civilization—those were already enough to prevent a second extinction. Probably the original extinction was caused by a complicated combination of many factors. But we've ended poverty, racism, war, the previous humans' environmental destruction of the planet . . . surely that's enough. Surely if there was anything else your generation needed to do, they would have given you those instructions in the awakening video."

Nick glanced quickly back at the other grown-ups—they were all nodding as if they completely agreed with what Mom was saying. As if none of the others could read the guilty secrets on Nick's and Eryn's faces, either.

"You understand that we had to look, though, don't you, Mom?" Eryn asked, and Nick could tell that she was trying to sound chastised and humbled.

Trying to fake it.

"Yes, but this has gone far enough," Mom said sternly. "Promise me you're done now. Promise me you won't put yourselves or anyone else in any more danger, looking for reasons for the extinction."

"I promise," Eryn said, hanging her head.

"Me too," Nick said, because what did it matter? They didn't have to look for reasons they already knew.

Now he let himself glance at Eryn, and he hoped she could read a different promise on his face: *I promise I won't say anything about the papers if you don't. We have to keep this secret. And then we have to . . .*

He wasn't sure what other promises he needed to make.

"Look, it's been a long night, after a long day—and a long week," Dad said. "Why don't we get out of this dangerous cave and go grab a few more hours of sleep before morning. We can leave any discussions about punishment for tomorrow. We'll figure out how you can make this up to us then."

"Sounds good," Mom said, standing and turning back toward the door.

That's it? Nick thought. *That's all they're going to say?*

Maybe they'd been programmed not to have any curiosity about the extinction; maybe that was programming they couldn't fight.

But shouldn't they, if that parental imperative thing makes them want to keep us out of danger? Nick thought.

Maybe not wondering about the extinction was an even higher imperative, one *they* didn't even know they had.

And . . . were they programmed somehow to raise us to think negative things about robots? Nick wondered. *Is that why, from the first time I saw wires sticking out of a human-looking body, I was disgusted? Is it like I've kind of been programmed too?*

He didn't know. He felt like he didn't know anything. His thoughts twisted around so much they were practically in knots.

He realized that Eryn had already stood up. She reached down to give him a hand up. And under the cover of reaching for him, she whispered, "We don't have to tell them anything, because we aren't killing anyone. We aren't like that. We'll find some other way."

Nick felt a pulse of gratitude to his sister for saying that, for spelling out the ground rules. *Their* imperative. It was something to hold on to, even as everything else confused him.

Mom turned and put an arm around Eryn's shoulders, and as they stepped out the door, Dad did the same to Nick. Eryn kept her hand on Nick's arm. For a moment the four of them walked like that, all of them linked together. Maybe kids whose parents had stayed married walked like that with their families all the time, but for Nick it was something new.

For a split second he could almost imagine they were just an ordinary family—everyone human, his parents still happily married. But then Mom let go of Eryn to turn off the light and shut the door, and Eryn let go of Nick to pull out her flashlight. In the dim glow of the flashlight beam, he could see Michael, Ava, Jackson, and Brenda ahead of him walking together, exactly the same way, and they looked even more like an ordinary happy family.

And they were all robots. Robots who had violated their programming, robots who didn't even have the right programming—robots who had already proved they could break and act unpredictably.

We won't have to kill anybody, Nick reminded himself. *We won't. We'll figure out some other solution. We will.*

He just didn't know what that solution could possibly be.

EPILOGUE

Jackson walked carefully, sandwiched between his mother and his sister. He tried to keep his thoughts just as confined. His brain had been fritzing out a lot lately, and he knew if it happened again here, in a dangerous cave, his parents would totally freak out.

Also, he didn't want to make a fool of himself in front of those other kids, Eryn and Nick. His stepsiblings.

The *real* humans. The ones who . . .

Don't think about that, he told himself, swinging away from panic like someone barely avoiding a cliff. *Think about . . . limestone. Sandstone. The beauty of a cave biome.*

He knew that he and his sister, Ava, were the only ones who could actually see the cave around them right now. Dad had programmed them to have only ordinary vision, just like anyone else, but Jackson and his sister had figured out how to upgrade their eyes—even giving themselves the ability to see in the dark. It had been easy.

But now, while the others clutched flashlights and still stumbled constantly, he knew better than to brag about his own skills. He knew not to say, *Take a look at the veining in that rock!*

He also knew not to say, *Was I the only one who saw those papers Eryn and Nick hid from us as soon as they saw us coming in that door? Was I the only one who read what was written on those papers? About how . . . how . . .*

Jackson's knees started to buckle.

No! No! Stop thinking about it! His brain screamed at him. Or, he screamed silently at his own brain. He was never quite sure which way it worked. His brain—or possibly his own self—screamed back at him, *I can't stop thinking about that! I have to do something! If anyone else sees those words, if Eryn and Nick decide to obey them, I have to . . .*

Jackson's body pitched forward. Ava and Mom grabbed for him, but it was too late. His inner circuits sizzled and zapped. He felt his mind blanking out.

His last thought was, *It's okay. I can think about this later. I won't forget. I'll figure out how to handle this.*

There was still time to fix everything.

There had to be.

ACKNOWLEDGMENTS

Thank you to my sister's family—Janet, Robert, Will, Jenna, and Megan Terrell—for acting as consultants on certain aspects of this book.

Thank you to my friends Linda Gerber, Erin MacLellan, Jenny Patton, Nancy Roe Pimm, Amjed Qamar, and Linda Stanek for reading early versions of parts of this book and offering helpful advice.

Thank you to Sharon McCubbins, school media librarian at Cumberland Trace Elementary School in Bowling Green, Kentucky; and Violet Fairweather and Alecia Marcum, librarian and former librarian at William H. Natcher Elementary School, also in Bowling Green. When they invited me to speak at their schools—and then my visit came soon after a nearby sinkhole swallowed up eight Corvettes—they gave me a good idea for where to locate an important scene in this book.

And, as always, thank you to my agent, Tracey Adams, and my editor, David Gale, and everyone else at Simon & Schuster for their help.